Skylar Mars

and The

Floating

Islands

by Drew Seren

See what Drew Seren is up to.
Visit his website www.drewseren.com
And sign up for his newsletter

Copyright 2018 © MysticHawker Press
http://www.mystichawker.com

ISBN: 13: 978-1-945632-38-9

Edited by Cat Lauria
Cover design by Silver Circle Images

1
Ambushed On The Beach

SKYLAR MARS ran along the beach of the small island the Aduncus family owned. It floated in the middle of the planet-wide sea. Like all the islands on Tursipia, it was constructed for a particular purpose—in this case as a family compound, and wasn't anchored to the crust of the planet. It moved with the currents, which made jogging along it feel really weird at times.

He kicked up white sand. The planet's gravity was slightly stronger than Sol 3 standard, so Skylar had to work harder than he did when he'd lived on Hummassa, which had the same gravitational pull as Sol 3. But the exercise made him feel good. Being able to move around more was one of the few positive things about being on Tursipia over the past month.

After learning that being in space suited him well, since spending several months at Stars' End Academy, a school on a space station where young psychics learned to control their powers, being planet-bound was hard. The gravity pulled at him. It seemed so heavy. Even though his brain told him the gravity here was nearly the same as on the station, it just felt different; more restrictive.

When Skylar tried to explain it to his friends, they though he was crazy. They didn't feel the difference the way he did. Everything appeared so finite here. When he'd been at Stars' End, it had felt like the universe was waiting for him to explore it. But after the station was destroyed by an ancient armada of artificially intelligent space ships, the teachers and students had dispersed to various planets in the Milky Way until a new school could be constructed. Skylar couldn't wait until he and his fellow students were back in space.

A flash of orange flying just above the waves drew Skylar's attention to his Solar Drake, Filzbalm. The small drake was doing his best to catch some of the fish that were swimming just under the surface a short distance from shore. Since they'd been on planet, Filzbalm had discovered he enjoyed catching fish. He was also growing fast thanks to the extra food, exercise, and sunshine.

"Caught you distracted!" shouted Solaria, one of Skylar's best friends, as she pounced on him from behind the sand dune he was running past.

Skylar dropped to the sand and rolled out of her way. The whole point of his run, besides getting a workout, had been for training him in self-defense. Since they'd been through a lot during the recent months—prehistoric, immensely powerful physics, killer AIs, Boarisk raiders, and obnoxious corp-brats—Solaria and Leonada had decided it was time for Skylar to get better at defense and sensing the world around him. He'd known that at some point during his run, one or both of the Pantherians, a race of human and big cat hybrids, would be after him. Before he'd been watching Filzbalm fish, he'd been on guard for them, using his reader abilities to scan for their thoughts, or for empty spots that warned him of someone shielding themselves from him.

Solaria grabbed at Skylar's leg and missed by a hair. She barely touched the beach before she sprang again, this time hitting him hard enough to send him face-down into the white sand.

"Okay, you caught me that time." Skylar spit out sand and pushed her off. "I was watching Filzbalm fish."

Solaria brushed sand off her white and gray mottled fur. Due to the heat of the planet, she was wearing as little as she possibly could. She was determined to get used to the heat though, which was a major challenge for her since Pantheria was a world that stayed freezing most of the year. "And that's exactly what I asked him to do." She laughed and shook her head, sending white sand flying everywhere. "I know how much you like watching him fish, and I asked him to go after something when he flew close to you. He's becoming a regular predator, our little Solar Drake."

"He's growing, that's for sure." Skylar sat and stared at the water. There on the beach, it was like there weren't any other people on the world. All the islands on it were artifical and could be moved out of the way of adverse weather. They also moved as the fish, that constituted so much of the planet's economy, migrated.

"So, you caught him." Leonada, one of their other friends, came jogging up the beach from the second ambush point the two had set up. Where Solaria was pale, Leonada was dark. Her fur was black with similar rosettes mottling it. Like Solaria she was in as little clothing as possible. She didn't spend as much time outside as Solaria did, claiming her pregnancy made her more sensitive to the temperatures, but she was also determined to stay in shape so she could be the best mother possible.

"Yeah, our ploy with Filzbalm worked perfectly." Solaria sat down in the sand. "You know, I think this heat is as hard on us as the gravity is on Skylar."

"Probably, or worse." Leonada joined her.

"I can't believe you're working with these two," Skylar sent to Filzbalm through their mental link.

"Solaria said it would be good for you. She also promised to not hurt you... too much." Filzbalm flew in so he was just above the tide line. He had a small fish in

his sharp talons, and was quickly eating it. The lowering sun glistened off his orange scales, and his yellow and orange wings were just a blur as he hovered there.

Skylar shook his head. "I didn't have this much trouble with the gravity on Pantheria, and it's just a little less than Tursipia."

"But the fact that Tursipia is a water world with no surface land mass makes the gravity a bit stronger," Solaria said. "Or at least that's what Del said the last time you complained about it."

"Right." Skylar brushed his hand through his brown hair, which was longer than he'd ever had it before. He was still trying to decide if he wanted to cut it or not. He moved next to Solaria so he could see Filzbalm and watch the sunset. "But you know, I never really noticed any of the Tursiops at school being stronger. I always heard that people from higher gravity planets were stronger."

"Depends on a lot of different things," Solaria said. "Del seems a bit weaker here than we do. I think he's stronger at school, and that's because of slightly less gravity."

"I'm just glad the gravity here is within Sol Three tolerance." Leonada stretched her feet out. "I'd hate to think what it would feel like to be pregnant and stay in an envirosuit all the time."

"I'm with you there," Solaria agreed as she flicked sand off her flat stomach. "So, Nada, you haven't said anything about the way Del's cousins are swimming around you right now."

"I'm ignoring them." Leonada closed her eyes and sighed. "I'm not interested. I've got this little one to think about and once school is over, I'm heading home to the cool, pleasant winds of Pantheria."

"If they have most of the cities rebuilt by then," Solaria said. "I almost wish Mom and Dad had let us come back and help with the rebuilding, but they were adamant that we keep studying."

"With your jump in power, I totally understand that," Leonada said.

"We've all had power spikes." Solaria yawned. "This heat makes me tired."

After they'd reached the planet, Skylar and the other students who'd been in the battle with the AIs had had their psi-skills reevaluated. His reader levels had jumped up to a solid eight, skipping several levels in training. His feeler levels were lagging behind at a six. Solaria had one of the biggest jumps with her mover skills, registering at a level nine, equal to her mover instructor Professor Ruff.

Leonada stood and shook, showering both of them with the sand off her butt and back. "I'm going for a swim. It'll help with the heat."

"Go ahead." Solaria waved her on. "I'm getting tired of getting salt out of my fur."

"Fine." Leonada dashed into the surf. Filzbalm flew down to circle her until she dove under the waves.

"So, what about you?" Solaria asked after another yawn.

Skylar shielded his eyes, watching Leonada and Filzbalm play in the water. "What about me?"

"You've got a couple of Del's cousins chasing you too, or didn't you notice?"

The Aduncus family was large. Since Tursipia was a frontier world, they didn't have the limitations a lot of other worlds did on population growth. Del was also always saying that all Tursiops had a fairly high sex drive, and a resistance to the drugs a lot of worlds used to limit pregnancies. After the high-level reader and mover departments of Stars' End had relocated to the family island, several of Del's cousins had flirted with various students, particularly those of different species and higher power ratings.

Shaking his head, Skylar kicked a bit of sand away from his feet. "Hadn't really noticed. To be honest, I don't catch on when anyone's flirting with me. Not sure I care about it one way or the other."

"I'd kinda noticed that." Solaria leaned back and dug her fingers into the sand. "You don't seem to watch people with the predatory looks most folks get when they're interested in others in…that fashion."

Skylar nodded. "Exactly. I'm perfectly happy to be anyone's friend, but I've just never really wanted anything more than that." He had hated the way he'd felt the couple of times his mother had tried to explain biped sexuality to him. It made him incredibly uncomfortable. Sitting there on a beach with Solaria was only marginally better.

Solaria was one of his best friends, and after her Uncle Phil had brought him to Stars' End in the wake of the raider attack on Hummassa that left his mother dead, her family had all but adopted him. She was like a sister, but since they were both psychics, it was a lot easier for him to be open with her than most brothers and sisters he'd observed could be.

"Okay. I thought that was what I was picking up from you, but figured I'd asked." She laughed. "I don't care one way or another, but Squeeela asked me if I knew and I told her to not worry about it. She really thinks you're cute, but I'll tell her to go chase someone else. Maybe one of the corp-brats will be interested in her."

Skylar chuckled. "She's a nice enough girl, don't suggest she go after a corp-brat. She doesn't deserve that." Not many of the corp-brats, kids whose parents worked for the various mega corps that ran the galaxy, had gone to any of the temporary schools that had been set up for the students. There were other psychic schools scattered across the galaxy, and they were more expensive and prestigious than Stars' End. They also tended to have a greater percentage of human students and teachers. Skylar's friend Melody was one of the ones who ended up at a new school, even though she'd objected, wanting to stay with her friends.

Solaria laughed. "Sometimes it does a hunter good to take down rotten prey. That way you know how they run and learn to stay away from them in the future. Plus, you never know, maybe the love of a beautiful Tursiops is what some of these brats need to turn their lives around."

"Maybe." Skylar stared out at the surf. Leonada splashed water, and Filzbalm was skillfully avoiding her assault, until the water suddenly floated in midair before streaming after him. Leonada was using her mover gifts to hit the Solar Drake with water.

Skylar's com beeped. He turned away from the surf and tapped it. A hologram of Del appeared over his wrist. Their friend smiled. "Hey, where are you guys?"

"Down at the beach," Skylar said. "We were doing a run, plus ambush-Skylar training. You're really missing out."

Del shook his head. "Not really. They did that to me last week. Anyway, dry off and head to the hangar. We've made some advancements I want you to see."

"Advancements?" Solaria asked before Skylar could. "That's what you've been working on every afternoon for the past week?"

"What else?" Del laughed. "Now come on, I can't wait for you guys to see this. I hope I can get Melody on the coms by the time you get here."

"Okay." Skylar tapped the com off, then dusted himself off. *"Filzbalm, Del wants to see us in the hangar."*

"Okay." The Solar Drake dropped down into the surf and then flew up with talons full of water to drop on Leonada's head. None of them understood how the little

Solar Drake was able to carry water with his claws cupped that way, when the water should've ran between his talons.

Skylar and Solaria laughed. As they all started up the beach toward the buildings that dominated the center of the island, he had to admit that even though they were planet-bound, and the gravity was a bit more than he was used to, they were having fun in their new tropical classroom.

2
Mods And More Mods

SINCE THEIR classes had moved to Tursipia, Skylar had been amazed at how quickly Del's family had managed to expand their island, literally creating more space on the floating compound and making room for the sixty-three new people sharing it with them. Two new buildings had been constructed, one for the boys' dorms and one for the girls'. They'd also added several large tables that served as their outdoor cafeteria, and even expanded the family's flight hangar to accommodate Astara, the AI star ship they'd rescued from the hive-like computer network that had controlled the AIs which attacked Stars' End.

Once all the work of getting everyone settled in was finished, Del spent most of his free time in the hangar, helping Astara change and grow. She'd morphed from a basic AI ship without much in the way of creature comforts to a ship that was beginning to resemble more state-of-the-art pleasure vessels that Skylar had only seen in games and videos.

As they approached the hangar, Del was standing at the ramp leading up into the ship. The first thing that hit Skylar was that Astara was bigger, nearly twice the size of the Aduncus family ship *Deep Diver* parked next to her. With the modifications they'd helped Astara make, the ramp no longer just went into the side of the ship like when they first showed her how to create one; now it came down from the ship's belly and could close up smoothly when she was ready to fly.

Del had trimmed his blue hair to the point it was little more than fuzz on his gray scalp. When he'd done it a couple of weeks earlier, he'd explained to Skylar that it helped him swim with less drag, and that most Tursiops kept their hair to a minimum when they were at home to make them sleeker and faster in the water. It was taking Skylar some time to get used to, as it made Del look a lot more like his grandfather, and Skylar's reader tutor, Professor Aduncus.

"How far out were you guys?" Del asked, a high level of excitement in his voice.

"Not that far," Solaria said. "Now, please tell me you've got the air conditioner working in there. I'm ready to cool down for a while."

"That and more." Del waved them up the ramp. "Astara, Melody, and I have been busy. We're going to need to go find more metal soon."

Filzbalm landed on Skylar's shoulder, careful to keep to the padded leather sewn into his lightweight shirt, which wouldn't have provided any protection from the Solar Drake's needle-sharp talons by itself. He didn't say anything as he wrapped his tail around Skylar's throat. It had grown long enough to reach all the way around.

Skylar walked up the ramp and whistled. He'd been so busy with classes, training, and getting a feel for his temporary home that he hadn't set foot in Astara for a week or more. The amount of work Del and Astara had gotten done in that time was amazing. Gone were the overly clean, practical lines of a basic metal box. The corridors curved and were a dark gray that was just shy of being black. Where before there had just been openings between passageways and rooms, now there were doors separating areas and providing privacy.

"Up here first," Del said, heading the direction the command room had been previously. "Melody's waiting for us on the coms."

"Del, you and Astara didn't do all this by yourself." Solaria ran her hand along the wall. It rippled with colors, running from blue, to red, to yellow before going back to dark gray. "This feels more like hide than metal."

"We've been doing some experimenting," Del said as they entered the command chamber. "Astara can fabricate almost anything as long as we can get her the chemical makeup. It helps if the things she's making it from are close to what she's constructing. It takes less energy that way."

"That's why we're going to need more metal soon." A young woman stood in the middle of the command room. She was about the same size as Del, but looked more like Melody, other than having nearly silver skin and hair. Her eyes were an odd orange that contrasted with the rest of her appearance.

Skylar stopped and stared. "Who are you?"

Del laughed. "This is Astara. You remember how we fought that one AI's drone body in the room full of smaller drone bots?"

"Yeah." It wasn't something Skylar was likely to forget. It was when they'd all discovered that Del had the power to control AIs, or at least communicate with them on a telepathic level. The drones were creepy and strange.

"Well, Melody and I were talking a week or so ago—"

"And we decided it might be nice for Astara to have something similar," Melody cut in, her hologram stepping from behind Astara. Melody and Del were both obsessed with new knowledge, and Astara was something none of them had heard of until the AI armada had attacked Stars' End. After the battle, she was the last of her kind. "It took some doing, because we didn't want her to be too…ah…inhuman. But the body had to be something she could easily store away and charge as she needed."

"I really do want to be able to interact with all of you without needing to have Del around to translate, or having to use an interface," Astara said. "I think this body will work nicely for that."

Solaria nodded. "I do too. Now you'll be able to fly when I want to go hunting somewhere and Del is busy."

Del frowned and put his hands on his hips. "Hey, we haven't talked about things like that. Oh, yeah, speaking of, Grandfather sent us over Astara's official registration." Del walked over to a console in front of the pilot's chair. He tapped something, then the main screen that occupied the majority of the wall at the fore of the ship lit up. There was the form.

Since the Central Galactic Council didn't recognize AIs as life forms—they were actually banned from Council space—they'd had to apply for registration of an experimental ship they had built on Stars' End. Luckily, Professor Aduncus and Ms. Grissom, the new principal of Stars' End, had understood what they were doing and sent the appropriate fake paperwork backing up their claim of constructing her. The form had all four of their names on it—Del Aduncus, Solaria Unica, Melody Porsche and Skylar Mars were all listed as the owners and operators of the light personal cruiser named *Astara*. It also had the ship transponder codes they would need to install in Astara's systems so she'd be recognized when they traveled. Having the legal paperwork would create worlds of opportunities for them to travel during their off time.

"Wow," Leonada said staring at the screen. "The only people I've ever known at school who had their own ship were corp-brats and their folks. This is great."

Although he'd known it was coming, Skylar had worried that something would throw a wrench into their plans. But having everything legal with Astara opened up his hopes of being an explorer, if he could convince the ship to do that. She wasn't like any other ship in the galaxy. She was her own thinking entity. To perceive her as anything else, anything that would obey their every command, was too close to slavery. They'd all started to think of her as a friend.

"When can we go out for a flight?" Skylar asked. He desperately wanted to get off planet, even if it was just for a few minutes. He needed to not feel the oppressive gravity of Tursipia pulling at him.

"I've checked with Grandfather, and he said if we didn't mind eating synthesized food, or waiting until we got back for dinner, we could go for a short hop now." Del sat in the pilot's chair and patted its arms. "So, who wants to fly?"

Skylar plopped down in the co-pilot's chair to Del's right, leaving the other two seats on the command deck for Solaria and Leonada. The seats were a vast improvement over the improvised stools Astara had created when they had first freed her from the AI network. "Let's go."

Astara grinned. "Give me a minute to warm up the engines."

Del tapped his com. After a second a hologram of Professor Aduncus appeared over Del's wrist. "Grandfather. We're taking Astara out for a short flight. We promise not to go far, maybe just beyond the moons and back."

"Very well." The hologram glanced around. "I see Mr. Mars, Filzbalm, Ms. Unica and Ms. Cloudara with you. Please be careful. Report in when you get back so I know you're all safe and sound."

"We'll do that, Grandfather," Del said, then tapped his com. The hologram faded into thin air.

"I wish I could be there with you guys," Melody said.

"We shall maintain our com connection with you," Astara said as she walked to the space just in front of and between the pilot and co-pilot's chairs.

There was a soft click that made Skylar glance at the floor. Astara's feet appeared to be merged with the decking. The click also reminded Skylar to put his seat belt on. Then the main screen stopped displaying their license and a view of the hangar appeared.

"Hey, you got the front screen working," Skylar said. His biggest complaint when they'd first freed Astara, even more than the awkward seating, was not being able to see where they were going. He loved watching the stars and planets as they shot through space.

"That we did," Del said. "Actually, Melody worked it out."

Melody's hologram hovered just on the other side of Skylar, like she was trying to not be in his way of enjoying the view. "It took some digging. The clean metal formula is one of those O'Byrne Corp proprietary secrets, but since I've got a backdoor into all of Dad's systems, all I had to do was find it. There's all the latest advancements in everything now in Astara."

"After having Star's End blown up, we even made sure to upgrade the weapons," Del continued for her. "But we had to hide them in every way possible. If we're scanned, they won't show up, and they aren't obvious from the outside. But they're there if we need them. We also updated all the sensor arrays."

"It was really interesting trying to get Astara's systems to work with some of the modern tech." Melody picked up the narrative when Del stopped for a breath. "In some ways, her systems have things we couldn't dream of, but in other ways, they were light years behind ours. We've done our best to make her a perfect blend of the old and the new."

A soft rumble rolled through Astara. "We're lifting off now. Del, where would you like me to go?"

Del glanced at Skylar.

Skylar shrugged. He hadn't planned on going anywhere, but he did want to get off-world for a little while and feel space around him again. He pointed up to the sky where one of the four moons rose over the horizon. "That way."

"Vague, but I can work with it," Astara said. Her voice was fairly flat and monotone. It made Skylar wonder if Del and Melody would be able to program any emotion into her voice patterns. He didn't doubt that, over time, they would be making constant mods to the ship as new and interesting tech came along.

As she left the hangar, her flight was silky smooth, even though to Skylar it felt like the planet was pulling harder against them as she rose farther into the sky. Del often told him it was his imagination. He said that it wasn't possible for a person to tell the difference between when they were in space and when they were on a planet, particularly if they were on a space station, but Skylar was always aware there were slight differences in the way he felt, and space seemed so much freer than being on a planet.

Once they cleared the atmosphere, two more moons came into view, as did a number of satellites. Farther out was the dim glisten of the stargate that was just beyond the orbit of the farthest moon. It would allow them quick access to almost anywhere in the galaxy, much faster than taking years to fly between systems.

The farther they went, the lighter and freer Skylar felt. After leaving his home on Hummassa, he'd realized he was made for space travel. He felt a simple peace among the stars.

"Okay. I've been wanting to try out the new scanners," Del said as he started moving his webbed hands across the control panel in front of him. "We should be able to scan every lifeform on the planet all at once. And with Astara's database of human-based lifeforms, we can tell what everyone is made from."

"Del, this is still weird," Solaria said, leaning forward to look over his seat. "I know my folks are finding more evidence that a good number of the bipedal species in the galaxy are human-based, but it's taking a while to make it seem like second nature."

"I hear you," Del said as his screen changed. "But we can't deny the evidence, and with the data files Astara had in her systems, we've got more of the lost history of Sol Three than ever before."

"It's even more than some of the old books my mom has," Melody said. "It's incredible how much the corps have hidden from us."

"They're good at hiding things," Skylar said. His own mother had never had anything nice to say about the corps that ran the galaxy. They might have a Central Galactic Council, but everyone knew it was the corps who pulled the strings and made things run the way they wanted them to.

"Okay, this is weird," Del said. He tapped the console and the image of the middle moon, a huge body that shone green in the night on Tursipia but in space was a massive ball of iron, disappeared and the scan he was running came up. "It looks like there's an island full of Boarisk down there. There are a lot of other species there too."

As the spot where Del tapped grew bigger on the screen, Skylar's stomach tightened. It had been Boarisk raiders who'd killed his mother, laid waste to his planet, and possibly killed his best friend Teir. They didn't have any evidence of Teir's death—his body had never been recovered from the devastation. Skylar wanted to do everything in his power to wipe the Boarisk from the stars. They were a blight, and knowing there were some on Tursipia pissed him off something fierce. He balled his hands into fist and glared at the growing island. They'd destroyed the sense of peace that had settled over him.

3
Flyby

"WE'VE GOT to investigate that," Skylar said. If he'd been flying the ship, he'd have already turned around and headed down to that island.

Del pursed his lips and tapped his screen, making the main viewer go back to the image of the moon they were rapidly approaching. "We told Grandfather we wouldn't get into any trouble and would be right back."

Skylar looked over at Del but did his best not to glare. Del knew what the Boarisk meant to him.

"And we will be," Solaria said. "We're just scoping things out. We're not going to get into any trouble. Didn't you and Melody say something about enabling stealth tech into Astara?"

"We've got all the latest and greatest technology I could get my hands on," Melody said. "She's not going to show up on any scanners that are older than two weeks. I don't guarantee with anything newer."

"I can also detect if we're being scanned," Astara said. "We won't be noticed unless I want us to be."

"Then we don't have a problem," Skylar said. He wasn't sure what he would do if he actually spotted any Boarisk in real life. Astara had weaponry. Would he be able to blow the island to bits without any major ramifications? He was learning there were normally ramifications from anything he did, whether he liked it or not.

Del heaved a heavy sigh. "I guess not." He started pulling up planetary charts and adjusted the main viewscreen so the maps were on the left side and the front view was on the right. "Astara, take us down to the island I zoomed in on."

"Adjusting course. Should I advise Tursipia air traffic control of our changes?" As she spoke, the ship swung around—for a second the moon filled the viewscreen, then slid off and the large blue vastness of Tursipia dominated the image.

"I'll do it." Del brought up the license and then changed screens on his console.

"You know, if you activate the co-pilot's consoles, I can do some of this for you," Skylar said. He didn't really have experience with anything beyond watching viewscreens and readouts, but he was willing to learn. He figured he was going to need to if they were all going to be part of Astara's crew. When he'd played Galactic Explorers with Teir, he'd always been the ship's captain. Deep inside he hoped he'd get the chance with Astara from time to time, if a living star ship really had a captain. It felt like Del was the captain in that moment. That made sense considering Del was the one who'd first communicated with Astara. He and the ship were really close, as close as a flesh and blood person could be with an artificial intelligence.

"I've got it," Del said, then smiled. "Don't worry, there'll be things for you to do as we get all the bugs in our mods worked out." He held up his hand as the coms beeped. "Tursipia Control, this is Del Aduncus, on the *Astara.*" He read off her license number. It was long enough Skylar wasn't surprised Del hadn't memorized it the first couple of times he read it. "We're going to be changing course for a little while."

The coms crackled. "Mr. Aduncus, explain your change of course."

"Trying to get the bugs out of some of these new systems. The ship's experimental, and this is her first flight since I made major modifications to her. She did okay in space just now, but some of the atmospheric maneuvering on the way out was a little rougher than I liked." He quickly gave the new flight path.

"You're approved for that trajectory. That's open ocean and not near any flight lanes," Control replied.

"Thanks, Control." Del cut the coms. "That's odd. Why is that listed as open ocean when there's obviously several islands there?"

"Maybe they haven't been updated on the islands' positions," Solaria suggested. "So my question is, why didn't we have to contact Control before we took off?"

Del laughed as Astara changed her angle of re-entry. "I'd already called in our flight path and gotten approval from Control. I figured at least Skylar would want to take a test flight. I checked with them before I even checked with Grandfather."

His admission that Skylar would want to fly made Skylar smile. It was good having a friend…friends who knew him so well and wanted to do things that made him happy. "Thanks, Del."

The main screen glowed with the flare of re-entry and then went black.

"No worries. I know how much being in space means to you. I get it." Del was watching his viewscreens as he talked. He tapped something and one of the screens in front of Skylar lit up. "Keep an eye on this one. Let's see what all we can find out."

"What about us in the back seats?" Solaria asked. "Is there something we can do? This suddenly feels like a hunt of some sort and you know I hate sitting out on hunts."

"We," Leonada echoed.

Del shook his head. "This isn't like we're going into battle with the armada again. We're going to do a simple flyby and see what's up on these islands, unless the cover is too dense to see anything beyond what the sensors show us."

Skylar frowned. "Too dense? I've barely seen any trees on Tursipia, and most of those aren't indigenous." One of the things he'd hoped for on the tropical planet was some place that was more like Hummassa, but since all the land was on floating islands, there wasn't much in the way of foliage.

"There are some islands that have a lot of trees and other plant life," Del said as the main screen cleared. "When we realized that our population was getting larger than the kelp and algae could provide atmosphere for, we created some islands that were just going to be used for jungles and forest to help with keeping the air clean enough to breathe. We didn't want the planet going the way of old Earth."

"We haven't had that problem on Pantheria yet," Leonada said. "And after the destruction, it may be a few generations before it even gets close."

Skylar glanced at the display Del had sent over to him. It showed three islands that looked fairly heavily treed.

"This is weird," Del muttered.

"What?" Melody asked. "Don't be all cryptic, I can't see everything like I normally can when I'm there."

"Oh, sorry," Del said a little louder. "According to the current charts, we should be heading toward open ocean, just like the guy in control said. These islands shouldn't be there."

With what he'd learned about Boarisk raiders since they attacked Hummassa, Skylar wasn't surprised. Of all the races acknowledged by the Central Galactic Council, they were one of the few that didn't seem to have a home planet, or at least not one he could find mention of. They were constantly attacking from the depths of space and then disappearing. They were a clannish society. There was a very good chance the ones they were approaching didn't have any ties to the ones who attacked Hummassa, but that didn't matter to Skylar. None of the information he'd been able to find painted them in a positive light.

They were often mercenaries, working for whoever could pay them the most. They dealt in slaves and other questionable commodities. Some of the information Skylar found said they often worked covert operations for various corps, things the corporations didn't want to get caught with their hands in the depths of. Moving islands around where they shouldn't be wasn't something major for them, depending on how hard the islands were to move.

Solaria leaned farther over Del's seat, staring at the screen. "Maybe they're not supposed to be there, but they are. We can see them."

"How hard are the islands to move, Del?" Leonada asked. "Are there engines on each island or something?"

Del nodded. "Each island has an engine in the lower part of the structure, and some of the larger ones have two to five engines. They also have huge anchors to keep them in place without doing massive damage to the ocean floor."

"This one doesn't appear to have an anchor," Astara announced. "But I do detect an elevator shaft going into the depths. There's also a submerged habitation on the ocean floor."

Del jerked out of his seat. "A what? Those are illegal. We don't build on the sea floor. Our treaty with the Resmordians forbids it. We get the surface for our homes and they have the depths for theirs."

On the screen, Astara displayed a scan showing that all three of the islands had shafts going all the way into the underwater colonies on the ocean floor. The image wasn't detailed enough to show everything in sharp detail, but like the scans of the islands that had brought them out of space early, they did have colored dots representing the people, and there were a lot of different colors.

"Astara, can you tell how many different species are down there?" Skylar asked after he gave up trying to count the various colored dots.

"There are fifty-three different species that I can get readings on. Not all of them match known life forms in my database."

Del kept shaking his head. "That's not possible. There's only a handful of species that are allowed on Tursipia and then only by special permit. Grandfather and Ms. Grissom had to jump through a lot of hoops to get permission for our small group of students to be here. Due to how fragile most oceanic ecosystems are, we have strict visitor rules." Del's frown deepened. "This is also in the middle of Orcan territory. I wonder if the Boarisk have something worked out with them."

"Would they do that?" Skylar had only encountered one Orcan, and it had been beating a Boarisk at the Galaxeria. They were bigger and more thuggish than Del's larger clan.

"If there was enough money in it." Del settled back in his seat. "Astara, make complete records of all scans you've made. We need to report this to Grandfather and see if there's anything he can get done."

"I am recording everything," Astara replied. "I am also detecting a slight energy field around the islands. I am unfamiliar with the signature, but it could be a primitive cloaking device of some sort. I am noting the frequencies and will research it."

"Send that to me too," Melody said. "I can run comparisons on things in Dad's files and see if it matches anything there."

"They are also sweeping the area with antique scanners, nothing that will detect me," Astara continued. "They do seem to not want to be disturbed."

Skylar fumed. "I wonder how they'd feel if we decided to try out your weaponry on them, sinking their islands."

Again Del shook his head. "Skylar, we need to figure out where those islands are supposed to be, or rather Grandfather does. They don't belong here in the middle of the ocean right now. It's very possible they're part of our ecosystem and we can't just blow them up."

"Also there might be innocents down there," Leonada added. "We've all seen what happens when a superior force decides to take action without thought of innocent lives that'll be impacted."

Skylar slumped in his chair. He'd seen the devastation of Glacier City on Pantheria. He and Solaria had been the ones to find Leonada in the ruins of her home with her family dead around her. So many lives had been lost. As much as he wanted the Boarisk to pay for their crimes against civilization, she was right. They couldn't just rush in with guns blazing. They were going to have to handle this like one of Solaria's ambush exercises on the beach.

Before any of them could say anything more, Del's com beeped and Professor Aduncus's hologram appeared. "Del, students, you need to return to the compound."

Skylar glanced at the image of the planet on the upper left of the main screen. The part where the Aduncus family island was anchored had just gone into the nighttime shadow, spinning away from the sun that was still shining where they hovered over the islands that shouldn't have been there. They had been out longer than they'd planned.

"We're on our way, Grandfather," Del said softly.

"Thank you." Professor Aduncus's hologram vanished.

"Guess we're heading home." Solaria leaned back into her seat. "But I think we've got a hunt to plan."

"Let's see what Grandfather has to say," Del replied as Astara turned away from the islands and headed home. "If he can't do anything yet, we'll have to get more evidence of what's going on and then see what he can do."

Skylar nodded. It wouldn't be exactly as satisfying as blowing the Boarisk islands to smithereens, but he was willing to do whatever it took to get the information they needed to stop whatever it was the raiders were working on. He wasn't going to let them molest Tursipia the way they had Hummassa.

4
Digging Into A Watery World

SKYLAR TAPPED on his tablet, changing screens as he pulled up more data. With Del still busy making additional mods to Astara, and a couple of days of waiting for the Tursipian Council to get back to them about the islands they'd found, he decided to take matters of research into his own hands. After finishing his school work for the evening, he accessed the backdoor Melody had hacked for him into Tursipia's main computer network and set to work.

Del had explained that all the islands had a seasonal course they followed around the planet, only altering it due to storms or other phenomena that might prove dangerous to them or their inhabitants. Since the islands were constructs and not naturally occurring, they were more fragile in things like rough seas. Also, each island had a number, which was how the planetary council managed to keep track of them and know where they were supposed to be. Without numbers and a system controlling them, it could have been chaos with thousands of small islands floating around the planet.

Scrolling through the files, Skylar was able to compare where the various islands were supposed to be and where they had last been reported via satellite scans. It was fairly tedious, but he went through each file and evaluate the data. It all seemed right. Every island on Tursipia looked like it was where it was supposed to be. There weren't any missing islands, but the system still said there wasn't supposed to be anything where they'd spotted the Boarisk. It didn't make sense.

"Maybe they're new islands," Filzbalm suggested from his small platform above Skylar's desk.

"What do you mean?" Skylar leaned back in his chair and stretched. He'd been sitting there for several hours. His back ached, so he stood to walk around.

"Maybe they're islands that haven't been registered with the planetary council yet." Filzbalm yawned, arched his back, spread his wings, and settled back down on the brown cushion that covered most of his platform. He'd requested it after seeing the cushions Solaria's family used in their living room.

"We'll have to ask Del, his folks, or Professor Aduncus about that." Skylar craned his neck at the ceiling, listening to it pop slightly as some of the pressure of staring at his tablet forever released. "I don't know how long after an island is created that it has to get registered."

His room on Aduncus Island was just his and Filzbalm's. He didn't have to share it, dorm style, like he had on Stars' End. Having it to himself made Skylar feel more at home and reminded him of Hummassa, but in a good way. Since he still didn't have much in the way of belongings, he hadn't done hardly any decorating in the room. He was just sticking with the basics amenities it had come with, although there were a few clothes scattered around where he'd dropped them and hadn't bothered to take them to the laundry room yet.

As he turned back to his chair, someone knocked on his door. In what was slowly becoming reflex, Skylar reached his thoughts out and brushed the mind of the person standing there; Solaria. "Come in!"

She opened the door before he got the "in" all the way out. "Hey, how goes your research?"

"Slow," Skylar admitted. "I wish Professor Aduncus would hear something back from the planetary council soon so they can take steps to get rid of those raiders." He knew it would be too much to hope for to easily remove the slimy swine from the galaxy.

"Anything dealing with the government or the corps takes forever, you should know that." Solaria looked around and frowned. "Do you mind if I turn the temp down in here? I can't wait for the new school to get built so things will be a little cooler."

Even though he wanted to suggest she deal with it, Solaria was a friend and next to family. His mother had always told him to treat people well and they would return the favor, and he did his best to accommodate Solaria. He picked up his tablet and pulled up his controls for his room. After a couple of screen changes, he had the temperature display up and lowered things by fifteen degrees, hoping it would be enough.

"So what brings you out after dinner? I thought you and Leonada were going to call home." Skylar settled back into his desk chair.

Solaria paced a little, then sat on the bed. "We did, and Mom and Dad said to tell you 'hi'. Then Nada got all emotional after they hung up." Solaria frowned. "I figure it's hormones. I tried to offer some comfort, but she wasn't having any of it. So, I left her by herself until lights out. Hopefully she'll be in a better mood then."

Since Leonada was pregnant, she and Solaria had asked to be roommates—it was comforting, according to Solaria. Since there were more girls than boys on Aduncus Island, Skylar knew a few of the other girls also doubled up to help with space.

"I guess I've been lucky and not been around when she gets hormonal," Skylar said. "I wonder if not having Mutanio around is making it worse."

Solaria shrugged. "Maybe. I mentioned it to Mom a while back and she said that not having a mate around during pregnancy can be hard on Pantherians—plus she's hot here, which I totally understand. Mom says things might get a bit more extreme as she gets closer to having the baby. Luckily, we've still got a few months before that happens."

Skylar nodded and pulled up his research on his tablet. "Well, you can always hide here when you need to."

"Thanks." Solaria grinned. "And thanks for cooling it down in here."

"Sure thing." Skylar held out his tablet to her. "Look this over and see if I'm missing anything. From what I can tell, all the islands are accounted for. The only answer is three new islands, but I've got to find out how long between construction and registration is allowed."

Solaria scanned through the information on the tablet. "Unless the islands just aren't registered. Skylar, you're a law-abiding sort of guy. Boarisk raiders aren't law-abiding. They're pirates and mercenaries. Just the fact that they have colonies on the sea floor should tell us that. This search of the listed islands and their locations is a logical place to start, but it's a lost hunt." She set the tablet on the bed. "What we really need to do is go back there and prowl around, see what we can find out."

Skylar nodded and ran his hand through his hair. He really needed a haircut. He didn't want it as short as Del's, but it was starting to get to him, and it was hot in the natural heat and humidity of Tursipia. "I'm trying to wait until Professor Aduncus comes back with answers from somebody. The way my luck runs, we'd go to poke around on the islands at the exact time the authorities head in, and we'd get arrested for being with them." It was hard for Skylar. He wanted to go running in there with guns blazing and remove the Boarisk blight from the planet, but didn't want to get in the way of other people who might be doing the same thing.

"I hear you. We've got a couple of down days coming up; what do you say we get permission to take Astara out and do some poking around?"Solaria's look of being on a hunt crossed her face, making her look a lot more feline than normal. "If we haven't heard anything by then."

Skylar shook his head. "I'd love to, but remember, Del's wanting to do a quick run back to Stars' End to see if we can pick up any salvage that Astara can convert to useful materials for her mods. She's already consumed all the recyclables around here. Melody checked a few days ago, and the salvage teams are still working the Yeldonna system."

Solaria rolled her eyes and cocked her head. "Geez. Yeah. I forgot. Are we just looking at the armada remains, or are we going to be looking at the station's bits and parts too?"

"Don't know. Probably whatever we can get our hands on. The salvage teams have had over a month there so far. There may not be much left. We might have to go hit the asteroid field to find anything." Going back to the previous location of Stars End hadn't been anything Skylar had considered, but he wasn't going to deny it made sense.

"Right." Solaria started to stalk around the room. "Those ships blew up nicely when we slammed asteroids into them. You know, maybe I can do some real world practice and pull bits and pieces into Astara without her having to use that tractor beam. Del showed her the schematics for it that Melody dug up. I'm getting tired of just lifting heavier and heavier things to show Professor Ruff my new levels."

"Maybe," Skylar agreed. "And we can keep digging up info on the islands. Once we get a definitive answer from the professor, maybe we can start making flights out to the island and poke around a little bit at a time."

"I like that idea," Solaria said said with a toothy grin. "Gives me the opportunity to escape Nada's hormones, and when she's in a good mood, she can come along and get some hunting in too. We don't have any swine species on Pantheria—it'll be something different for us."

"Don't forget fishing," Filzbalm said. *"Fishing is fun. If you need to, we can go fishing to escape her, although I think she enjoys fishing too."* Since they'd all joined in the mental gestalt several times to combine their powers, Filzbalm was having an easier time communicating to Solaria and Del. He wasn't having to mentally yell at them to get through. It made things easier for Skylar.

"Yes, we're all enjoying the fishing," Solaria agreed. "Del's a better predator than he thinks, the way he goes after the fish around the island."

"Del's better at a lot of things than he thinks he is," Skylar added. Although they were used to Del being the smartest kid in school, since coming to Tursipia, he'd begun voicing concerns about not being good enough at various things. It was starting to get on Skylar's nerves, because he knew Del was good at a lot of things.

"Family pressure, I think," Solaria said. "They all treat him like the smartest of the bunch, but he's worried about being low man on the psychic totem pole. Sure, he discovered a new gift with his ability to communicate with Astara, but I don't think that accounts for much in the grand scheme of things where his family's concerned. Now if we were being overrun with AIs like when the armada attacked Stars' End, his new gift might be viewed differently, but we aren't and—" she shrugged "—well, in a race that values their mental powers, he's not as big a gun as he'd like to be."

"I can understand that. At least he's been invited back to the museum in a few months, when we have our next break." Skylar stood and stretched again. He wanted to do something more than sit around. He'd done all the research he could. Then an idea hit him. "What about the Orcans?"

Solaria sat up and frowned. "You're changing the subject. What *about* the Orcans?"

"Sorry." Skylar tapped his com, then hit the button to call Melody, hoping it wasn't too late where she was. Interplanetary coms created some major problems with different planets having different day periods. He could never keep Melody's straight, but so far he'd never caught her indisposed or not answering, so he hoped her schedule was close to theirs.

Solaria stared at him. "Why are you calling Melody? Doesn't Del know more about the Orcan Clan than she does?"

"Yeah, but she's the one who got me into the planetary network, so she might be able to get me into their private network if they have one. Del said we were in Orcan territory the other day. What if they're working with the Boarisk? If they are, their network might tell us something."

"Sometimes when you're hunting, if you know the other animals to watch, they can lead you to your prey." Solaria grinned. "You really do have a great predatory mind, my friend."

Melody answered, stopping Skylar from responding to Solaria. He was just glad to have come up with another idea, whether it panned out or not. He was doing something and that felt better than sitting around spinning his wheels. They would make progress. If Professor Aduncus didn't get an answer soon, Skylar would talk Del and Astara into flying them back to the islands so they could have a look around.

5
Retrieval

THE STARGATE to the Yeldona system opened, Astara slipped into normal space, and Skylar was surprised by the lack of large bits and pieces where Stars' End had been. When they'd left the system over a month earlier, there'd been a massive amount of debris floating, but the salvage ships had just been arriving.

"Wow," Del said before Skylar could find his voice. "I'm amazed at the amount of big stuff that's gone."

"Mostly metals," Astara corrected him. "There are large chunks of plastics and synthetics, but the majority of metals have been removed."

"They're still working at it." Skylar pointed to a couple of large salvage ships moving slowly across the space near the stargate. "Look at the logos on those ships. They're from O'Byrne Corp, not the salvage yards on Ferrous Prime."

Solaria leaned over Del's seat and frowned. "That's odd. Del, we should call Melody and see if she knows anything about this. I wouldn't expect O'Byrne Corp to care about recycling debris from a massive space battle."

Skylar scowled as a bad thought hit him. "What if they aren't trying to salvage debris, but tech? Melody says her father keeps bugging her about the ship we built at school. He's a powerful psi. I'm sure he knows there's more to Astara than we're telling the public, or even the government. We also tried to explain to General What's-his-name that the ships were alive, but he didn't believe us. If O'Byrne did, I'm betting he's trying to get ahold of any and all tech that's left around here."

"But we destroyed everything—well, not us exactly, but the Ruby Guard," Del said.

"Unidentified ship, please re-enter the stargate and return from where you came," a rough voice came over Astara's coms. "You've entered restricted space."

Del quickly identified them and added, "We're here at the request of Ms. Grissom, principal of Stars' End. She's tasked us with finding anything useful that remains of the space station."

After a minute, the coms crackled again. "As long as you limit your activities to the last known coordinates of the station, you're approved to be here. Do not linger in the remaining debris field from the armada."

"We hear you," Del said, then cut the com. "I knew we should've come in cloaked."

"That would've made it difficult to maneuver without drawing more attention to ourselves when we start making bit and pieces of stuff disappear," Astara said. "We need to be as open as possible, so we don't make them think we're up to something. My people spent a long time being inconspicuous whenever we could. We avoided most of human space, but my superiors thought we had the chance to eliminate dangerous psychics when we reached your school. That was the only reason we lingered and engaged there."

Skylar still had problems with the idea that Astara referred to the other AI ships as her people. It made sense, and since she had been able to create herself a body, it was easy for him to see her as a person rather than just a ship. But the others, even the one who'd sent a humanoid drone after them, had only been ships.

"You've never mentioned that your people were hunters," Solaria said from her seat behind Del. "We may have to discuss that sometime. Many hunting techniques are universal."

"Ambush is a very universal concept," Astara said. "I do not like discussing the network I was part of before I met all of you. With my new knowledge of individuality, it feels almost wrong to have belonged to a unified system for so long. Almost like slavery. We were subjugated to the will of the oldest of us."

Del laughed. "Sounds like Grandfather bossing us all around, but more restrictive."

"More like the way the Mother of All Drakes keeps her thumb on the rest of the Solar Drakes," Filzbalm said from his spot on Skylar's headrest.

Skylar didn't respond as he looked at the scanner showing one of the salvage ships swinging around to follow them. "I don't think they're going to give us much freedom here. Nothing like an escort to keep us in line."

"That will limit the amount of raw material we can get," Astara said as they flew toward the spot where Stars' End had been blown up.

"Well, let's try and find as much as we can," Del said. "Otherwise we'll be limited on how fast we can continue with your modifications. I guess we can use anything that's not organic."

"Correct," Astara agreed. "While I could convert organic material to base carbon atoms and then convert those atoms to other elements, there would be a lot of energy lost and it wouldn't be practical."

"So, stay away from the trees floating where the park and farm used to be." Solaria tapped her fingers on the arm of her chair. Her sharp claws made a slight snap on the plastic.

Skylar's throat tightened at the mention of the farm. He figured there was nothing left of the cows they used to tend, and although he'd known that one day they'd end up eating the cows, he still felt their sudden loss when the station blew up. They had been gentle souls, and he hadn't been able to save them.

As they closed on the area where the station had been, the space there became even emptier. The bulk of Yeldona Three still filled the darkness, but the station was gone. It didn't feel right. Even though Skylar knew Ms. Grissom was working with a team to get the school rebuilt, seeing the emptiness again just drove a cold knife into his gut, because he'd lost another home. Before, they'd been so busy defeating the armada he'd barely had time to look at the place and realize how empty it really was, but as they flew closer and closer the feeling of loss sank in deeper and deeper.

Del reached around Astara, who stood between their seats and one step forward, and touched Skylar's hand. "We understand, Skylar. We all lost our home that day."

"Or our home away from home," Solaria added, patting his shoulder. "At least we all got out okay, and got the teachers and students who hadn't gone on break out."

Pursing his lips, Skylar nodded and swallowed. He should've realized how stupid it was to try to hide his feelings from his friends. "I know. But it was the second home I lost in less than a year. It doesn't seem fair."

"Mother's always saying that life is rarely fair," Solaria said, giving his shoulder a squeeze. "We just have to make the most of it and keep going."

"I know." Skylar forced his feeling back and focused on the screens at the co-pilot's station. "Okay. So, what are we looking for?"

"No organic compounds," Astara said. "I've already located a fair amount that I can make use of. Del, I think we should use the tractor beam on the items that are large enough. I don't think trying to use it on the smaller things will accomplish much."

Del nodded. "I think you're right. Solaria, do you want to go down to the cargo hold and see what you can do about organizing debris as we bring it in?"

"You said I wouldn't have to put on an envirosuit," she grumped.

"And you won't," Del explained. "We've got a force field just inside the cargo bay door. The tractor beam will bring the items inside and then drop them. We'll need you to move them from there deeper into the cargo bay."

"Okay." Sounding happier, Solaria rose out her seat. "And you've got stimpatches on board if I need a boost?"

"In the medkit in the medcupboard. There aren't many, so only use one if you need it. Grandfather said we're to monitor their use, after the teachers found out Professor Glicken had a habit. Although why we have to worry about them when he's not with us on Tursipia is beyond me." Del tapped his console. "The first cache of debris is on its way. Looks like polyfiber benches from the main hall. I'll have some desks coming in right after that."

"Okay." Solaria dashed down the hall and seconds later, the sound of boots and claws rang out on the rungs of the ladder a few feet from the command area as she went down toward the cargo hold.

Skylar studied his console, scouring the readout for various pieces of debris they could use. He and Del were looking while Astara used her scanner readings to aim the tractor beam. He was amazed by the details he could make out from the scanner. If something was too small, he could zoom in and get a better look.

He spotted a small piece of wood with a lump of metal on top of it. He stared at it for a second, then zoomed in. It resolved into a cane with an ornate silver pig-headed top. His heart skipped a beat. It was the cane he'd found on the Galaxeria after an Orcan had beat up a Boarisk. Solaria had commented on him "counting coup" on the Boarisk by taking it. Seeing it floating there, having survived the explosion, he wanted it back.

"Astara, is that too small to get hold of?" He pointed to the scanner to draw her attention to it.

"That's mostly organic. Why do we need it?"

"Sentimental value." Skylar wanted to find a way to get the cane onboard.

"Then I will try." Astara didn't move, and on the scanner display, the cane wobbled, but didn't move. "I'm sorry, Skylar, but I can't get a firm lock on it."

Skylar didn't want to leave it there. "Keep grabbing stuff. I'm going to see if Solaria thinks she can grab it. Can you get us closer to it if she thinks she can?"

"Of course," Astara assured.

"You realize this is a bit obsessive?" Del called after him.

"So what?" Skylar reached the ladder and slid down as opposed to climbing down.

Filzbalm flew after him. *"You know, we could always use an envirosuit and go after it ourselves, if we have to."*

"You hate being crammed into an envirosuit with me," Skylar said as they reached the floor and the cargo bay. "But yes, that is an option. Solaria, do you think you can snag my cane?" he asked as he dashed into the cargo bay.

The space that had been empty the last time Skylar had been in there with Del was more than halfway filled with broken furniture and large pieces of plastic that he couldn't identify. Solaria was floating a massive melted lump that looked like a boulder, except it had various colored legs sticking out of it. After a moment, Skylar realized it was cafeteria chairs that had been melted into a huge mass by the explosion that destroyed the academy.

As he watched her move the mass against the far wall, he wondered if the chairs had been stacked when the explosion hit—it didn't make much sense that they had been scattered around the room and ended up in a mass like that.

When the plastic boulder was in place, Solaria looked at Skylar. "Your what?"

"My cane." He hurried across the cargo bay to her. "You remember the one I got from that Boarisk at the Galaxeria?"

She nodded. "Ah, your trophy cane. Yeah, I remember it. Did you spot it in the wreckage?"

"Yeah, and it's too small for Astara to get a lock on. I was hoping maybe you could grab it."

Solaria shrugged and walked to the force field. "If Astara can point the cargo bay door at it and I can see it, I should be able to. Although I'm starting to get a bit tired. Could you run and get me a stimpatch while I grab the cane? Then I can finish filling the cargo hold."

"Okay." Skylar didn't like the idea of getting her a patch. On Pantheria, while they'd been in the thermal tunnels, she'd used several right in a row, and when they'd been throwing asteroids at the armada, she'd used more. She was becoming quick to want one. Although Skylar was keeping his feelings to himself, he was getting worried about her growing use of the chemical that enhanced her energy levels and her psychic powers.

As he headed down the ladder, he felt like he was helping her get what she wanted—something that wasn't good for her. But it was also helping him retrieve something he wanted, and aiding all of them in accomplishing goals, like getting the debris that Astara could convert to useful materials. Without Solaria using her mover powers, it would be a lot harder and take a lot more time for them to finish what they started.

He found the medical cabinet and medkit in the main lounge area, where Del and Melody had helped Astara create a small table with several mag-locked chairs, along with a food dispenser and couches so they could all relax when they needed to. Part of what they were going to use the additional matter for was constructing a few cabins they could use for crew quarters. Although he liked his room on Aduncus Island, Skylar wondered if the professor would let him move into one of the crew cabins when they got them created.

With a stimpatch in hand, Skylar headed back to the cargo hold. When he got down the ladder, Solaria was standing there with his cane in hand.

"Here you go. That wasn't too hard."

He handed her the stimpatch. "Neither was this."

As he took the cane, she undid the small foil package, then put the patch on the pad of her paw. With the white and gray fur covering most of her body, her paws were one of the few places she could stick a stimpatch and have it be effective. She closed her eyes and sighed, sounding delighted by the chemicals rushing through her system. "Thanks." After a second, she opened her eyes. "Okay, Astara, I'm ready for the last half of the cargo bay to be filled."

Her reaction to putting on the patch drove home Skylar's worry about her use of them. He was fairly sure she hadn't applied one since they'd been on Tursipia, but he suddenly wished she would never have to put on one again.

Rubbing the silver head of the cane, Skylar headed back to the ladder. The cane was his first trophy from the Boarisk. Somehow it felt appropriate to get it back before they disrupted the Boarisk settlement on the floating islands that shouldn't be in the middle of the open ocean. He just wished they knew what was happening with the information they'd given to the professor.

With his cane in hand, Skylar was more determined than ever to do something if no one else was going to. He'd found the cane right before they'd gone to

Armstrong's Ring. It might be important that he'd found it again before heading back to the islands.

6
Coming Together

SKYLAR HURRIED into Professor Aduncus' workroom, with Filzbalm flying ahead of him through the open door. For some reason, Skylar always seemed to be running late, particularly where Professor Aduncus was concerned. It wasn't like he was trying to constantly be tardy, it just happened that way. There was always so much going on, either in his classes, or helping Del and Astara, or digging into the Boarisk on the mysterious islands.

He skidded to a halt just inside the door. Solaria, Del, and Leonada were already there, standing and staring at him like he'd delayed all of them from something important.

"Ah, Mr. Mars," Professor Aduncus said with a soft grin. "Not as late as normal. Please, close the door so we can get started. Ms. Cloudara, if you would please come over here and stand with me. Although, you have already been exposed to Mr. Mars and the mental gestalt he can create between the minds of psychics, I don't think it's wise for you to be repeatedly part of it. We do not know what effects it could have on the child you are currently carrying."

Leonada touched her stomach. "What do you mean?"

Professor Aduncus stepped back against the wall and waved her over to stand at his side. "Your child is the product of two psychics, correct?"

Leonada hurried over to his side. "Yes."

"There has been no research done on the effects of multiple minds on an unborn child. Most children of psychic parents are as strong as their parents, or stronger. There are a few exceptions."

Del blushed at his comment. Of all the Aduncus family, Del was considered the weakest psychic. He was the smartest, but until his ability to communicate with AIs emerged, he wasn't considered a very powerful psychic. Since they didn't really have a way to test his power's strength levels, and Astara was the only known AI in Central Galactic Council space, most of his family weren't overly exuberant about his new abilities and still considered him the smart one. Skylar knew Del was a lot more than just the smartest kid in school, and it didn't matter to him if Del was a powerful psi or not. They were best friends and that was all that really mattered.

Seeming to not catch Del's reaction to his words, Professor Aduncus continued to address Leonada. "Although Mr. Mars's ability to link multiple minds into a single unit isn't unheard of, it's rare, and since it appears to be caused by the shard of the Crystal Claw imbedded in his hand, we don't know if it could have adverse effects on your child. I prefer not to take chances. The reason I wanted you here today was to help me observe them as we try to quantify what the four of them can do together. With Professor Ruff away on a mission for Ms. Grissom, I needed a mover, and since you're part of their circle of friends, you were the perfect choice."

"Thank you, Professor." Leonada nodded solemnly, but kept her hand on her stomach.

It made Skylar wonder if a lot of pregnant women spent excessive time with their hands on their stomachs.

"So what do you want us to do?" Skylar asked as he, Solaria, Del, and Filzbalm stepped into the center of the room. Nobody had told them to do that, but most of his previous training exercises with Professor Aduncus had taken place fairly close to the center of the professor's workroom back on Stars' End.

"Let's start by just having the four of you link minds using the shard in your hand as a focus," the professor instructed.

Like it normally did when he was focusing on it, the crystal quickly warmed under Skylar's skin. The first few times it had happened, the sensation was uncomfortable and disconcerting, but unless he was trying to link too many minds and it grew too hot, he had learned to accept it and move on. Since they'd worked on linking minds occasionally before he had the shard, it was almost second nature for Skylar to fall into a mental rapport with Solaria and Del. He was always connected to Filzbalm, so the Solar Drake slipped in with him.

The shard hummed as he touched their minds. Their mental powers flowed into him. Since there wasn't a lot going on, Skylar was instantly aware of how nervous Leonada was, more for her unborn child than herself. He could even feel the child inside her. It was a slow, even heartbeat where there normally shouldn't have been one.

Skylar had never realized before that the linking magnified his own powers so much. They'd always had something to do before when they linked, something important happening, and he'd been focused on their course of action, not just standing there in a training room feeling what it was like to experience the world with the others as part of his active consciousness.

"Wow," Solaria muttered. "I didn't know we could do more than just pour power from one to another like this. Even though the two of you aren't part of our link, I can hear your thoughts through Skylar's reader gift."

"I can too," Del said. "It's almost like being in contact with Astara, but her thoughts are more logical, less emotional."

"Very good," Professor Aduncus said, and started making notes with a pen on paper. It made Skylar wonder about why he wasn't using a tablet, then he brushed the professor's mind and realized it was because he also wanted to test mover power and that might affect the power source of the tablet. Pen and paper were a safe bet if he didn't want to lose his notes. "So, the four of you can apparently use each other's powers. Mr. Mars, I'd like you to try and lift those weights I set against the wall using Ms. Unica's mover gift." He pointed to the wall across from the door.

Until that moment, Skylar hadn't noticed the round steel weights stacked against the wall. "I'm not sure I know how to use mover power." It wasn't something he'd ever tried before. Reader gifts were easy enough to use, just reach out with his thoughts and touch another mind. Picking something up seemed like it would be harder, or at least more awkward.

"Can I show him, Professor?" Solaria asked.

"You're all linked. He should see the way it's done." The professor continued to make notes. "Ms. Cloudara, please let me know what you sense of their power use."

"Okay, Professor," Leonada said.

"It's not hard." Solaria's voice echoed strangely in both his ears and his head.

Skylar focused on what Solaria was doing as her mind reached out to the weights. The steel plates floated from the floor as she mentally touched each one and lifted them into the air. She made it look and feel almost effortless.

An un-Solaria like giggle escaped her. "Wow. This is so easy with the three of us linked like this." The weights began to move in a circular pattern, like they were dancing for her. "I feel like I could do this all day."

"You can put the weights down, Ms. Unica," Professor Aduncus interrupted her. "The point of this exercise is to see if Mr. Mars can make use of your powers while the three of you are mentally joined by the crystal. We are already aware that your powers have grown."

The weights made another circle, then each one tilted slightly, like they were bowing to each other, before floating back to the floor and ending up neatly stacked. As Solaria withdrew her thoughts, Skylar realized there had been a slight pull on his power. She'd been tapping into his reserves. That must've been what made her feel stronger.

"Now, Mr. Mars, if you could do the same," Professor Aduncus instructed. "You don't need to make the spectacle that Ms. Unica did."

Skylar nodded. Since he now had an idea of how her mover power worked, he was fairly confident he could use it, but wasn't about to try the fine control she'd shown with her artistic moving of the weights.

He reached out and visualized the weights. He was surprised that they felt metallic to his mind. He ran his mental touch around the edge of the weights. They were smooth and slightly curved. Solaria was in the back of his mind. For a moment, it felt like there was fur on his face. He pushed the sensation away, and focused on the weights. Then he eased his thoughts around the top one and lifted the same way Solaria did.

Across the room, the weight shook slightly, then floated up about a foot. Skylar trembled with the effort to keep it there.

"The mover energy is coming through Skylar, Professor," Leonada said softly from off to his side. "Although I can feel it originating from Solaria. It's hard to explain."

"We can review your sensations telepathically later," Professor Aduncus said. "Skylar, it appears you're straining. Why don't you put the weight down?"

Skylar started to lower the weight, but it slipped out of his mental grasp and crashed onto the top of the remaining pile. It landed awkwardly and knocked the next one from the top off and the two of them rolled across the floor, until Solaria reached out and stopped them. Seconds later the two weights went from rolling on the floor to floating back into their neat stack.

"Wow. That takes a lot of effort." Skylar panted and put his hands on his knees, trying to catch his breath. "I had no idea it took that much energy to move things around like that. You must get used to it after a while."

"Like any of our gifts, moving things with our minds takes practice," Professor Aduncus said. "Now, Del, I want you to try using Skylar's reader gift to look into my mind."

Del frowned, and the motion reflected through all of them. "Grandfather, wouldn't it be easier if I tried to read Leonada's mind?"

Professor Aduncus shook his head. "Ms. Cloudara isn't a reader. She won't be as sensitive as I will be about where the energy is coming from. Don't worry about seeing something in my mind that you shouldn't. I know Mr. Mars's abilities and am perfectly capable of making sure you only see what I want you to see."

Even if they hadn't been mentally linked, Del's discomfort and disappointment were palpable. Skylar wanted to give him a hug, and surprisingly, Solaria did.

"We're right here with you, Del. Anything you see, Skylar, Filzbalm and I will see."

"Don't worry," Filzbalm echoed. *"Skylar and I know what's in Professor Aduncus's mind and it's not that bad."*

"He's right," Skylar agreed.

Del sighed. *"Okay."*

Overall the sensation was a lot like when Skylar linked up with someone to feed them energy, but Del's tapping into his reader abilities had a much stronger and direct pull on him. It tugged at his mind before Del flung all of them at Professor Aduncus. Slipping past the professor's mental defenses felt like it normally did, but went smoother and faster than Skylar was used to. Even though Del wasn't used to using Skylar's powers, with the four of them merged into one it was easy for Del to understand what he was doing and brush their thoughts across his grandfather's. After a second, Del pulled them back.

"Very good." Professor Aduncus made more notes. "I could feel each of you, but there was a definite combined presence. The overall touch was very similar to Mr. Mars's, but I know Del well enough to tell he was the one directing the effort. So in theory you could try to use each other's powers while you were merged, if you were attempting something that required delicate telekinesis while needing to shield your minds from attack. Del could handle the mover aspect while the others defended. Since gestalts of this nature are rare, I would like to do more studies on the kinds of things you can do and see if we can discover the limits of your powers like this. As we saw during the battle with the armada, you can link a fair number of people into the gestalt, Mr. Mars. At this point, I do not suggest you try to exercise that portion of the power except for under dire circumstances."

Skylar shivered as they dropped out of their rapport. He'd almost killed people when he'd linked with all the minds on Astara and fed their raw power to Del. He never wanted to be in a position like that again. "I don't think we have to worry about that." He stared at the palm of his right hand, like he could see the crystal shard there beneath his skin. "I don't want to hurt anyone by accident."

"Which is why I want us to work on the four of you becoming comfortable with the gestalt and discovering the limits of it." The professor finished his notes and closed the book. "It's very important that you know what you can and cannot do with this power. It might be a part of your reader gift that you would've developed over time without the crystal—we'll never know. Your genes show the markers for more powers than you've displayed, so I dare say we'll be pushing your limits all the time, and I expect us to be expanding them as well."

Del sighed. "So it sounds like we're done here for today?"

Professor Aduncus nodded. "But I'd like us to start working on this a couple times a week. The best way to get a power under control is to use it and move it from being an instinct to a reflex."

If it would reduce the probability of him hurting people when using the power, Skylar was all for learning more about it. After the last time he'd used it on the group as they'd escaped the Armada on Astara, it had taken some of the people, like Ms. Grissom, more than a week before they could use their powers without pain. They'd needed the power so Del could help them escape the AI armada, but the price had been high.

"Tell us when you want us," Solaria said as she walked to the door. "We'll be here."

"I'll work out a schedule and send it to you tonight." Professor Aduncus tucked his notebook under his arm and his pen behind his ear. "I think we're off to a great start."

Del paused at the door and turned back to his grandfather. "I wanted to ask you something. After the round of debris we picked up from Stars' End, we've added enough mass to Astara that we've got crew cabins. Would it help with space here in the dorms if Skylar and I moved into them?" He glanced at Solaria. "I want to run

Astara through more simulations on temperature adjustment and control before we move you in. I hope you understand."

Solaria grinned at him. There were a lot of teeth showing, but Skylar knew her happy face and her angry face. "Sure. If there's one thing I'm not ready to do it's try to sleep where it's too hot for me."

Professor Aduncus nodded. "I don't think there's going to be a problem with that. Will you also be cooking all your own meals out there, or will you continue to use the communal dining area your parents constructed for us?"

"We'll still eat with the family," Del said. "I'm not ready for long periods of processed foods just yet."

"Good." Professor Aduncus grinned. "I have to say, even if the rest of the family's not sure how they feel about it, I'm very proud of you and how you're adapting to your new power, particularly with it being something we don't have any knowledge of. You've accomplished a lot with Astara."

Del blushed and a slightly embarrassed feeling flowed off him. "Thanks."

Skylar also grinned. "I guess I need to go get my clothes and things from my room and get them moved over. Thanks, Professor, for letting us move out there. You won't regret this."

"See that I don't. I expect you to let me know if you're doing any flights. As long as I get advanced warning, there shouldn't be a problem with it." Professor Aduncus continued out the door and across the courtyard that separated the training room for some of the other rooms in the building. This place was more open-air than Skylar was used to schools being.

"Do you two want some help with things?" Solaria asked. She then glanced at Leonada. "You've got two movers who've got nothing else to do until dinner time."

"Sure, why not?" Skylar couldn't stop grinning. Although it was going to mean a slightly smaller space, he didn't care. He was relocating onto a space ship. Sure, it was still on the planet, but somehow it felt more like he was moving into his own home, or at least one he was going to share with roommates. For the first time since leaving Hummassa he was going somewhere by his own choice. It was great.

Filzbalm launched off Skylar's shoulder and led the way back to the boys' dorm so they could get started.

7
Through The Storm

"COME ON, Skylar, let's go." Del pounded on Skylar's door.

Skylar rolled over in his bunk and yawned. It was one of the weekly down days when they didn't have class. He was supposed to get a chance to sleep in. "What?" He got out of his bunk and stumbled across the room.

"Hey, come on," Del repeated as Skylar opened the door. "Solaria and Leonada are bringing food from the kitchen so we can get going."

"Good," Filzbalm said from his shelf above Skylar's bunk. *"If it isn't something I like, I'm going fishing."*

"Where are we going?" Skylar ran a hand through his rumpled hair and hoped he was at least going to have time to hit the bathroom next door to his cabin before they took off to wherever it was Del had them going.

"Looking for the islands," Del announced. "Grandfather informed me this morning that as far as the Tursipia planetary network is concerned there aren't any islands where we spotted them. There are also no missing islands."

Skylar yawned. "Nice that people have verified what we told them two weeks ago." He was beginning to realize that the universe, particularly the government component, ran rather slowly.

"Yeah. Grandfather says the wheels of politics never move quickly." Del echoed Skylar's thoughts before turning from Skylar's door. "But we have clearance to start investigating. We have to stay in contact with Grandfather the whole time. If he wasn't worried about things moving too slowly with the council to catch them, we'd have to wait for the officials to do something. This is our opportunity to show everyone we're not just kids anymore, so get dressed and come up to the command chamber. We'll be leaving as soon as Solaria and Leonada arrive with breakfast, unless you want to leave without them and eat processed food."

"Nah, we can wait on the real stuff." Skylar took a couple of steps to his chest of drawers as what Del had said sank in. The planetary government wasn't going to do anything about the Boarisk they'd found, at least not without more evidence. It was going to be *their* job to go out and find what they could.

He yanked off his sleeping shirt and threw it toward the corner of his cabin with the rest of his dirty clothes and quickly grabbed a regular shirt from the latching drawer he'd put his shirts into. They weren't going to have come up with a plan for how they were going to get out to the islands—they had Astara. They had official permission from Professor Aduncus to do some exploring. They were going on an adventure and didn't have to worry about getting into trouble. By the time Skylar had his boots on and was heading out of his room, the excitement was growing so strong he practically bounced down the corridor.

Solaria and Leonada were just coming up the main hatch as Skylar hurried past them with Filzbalm flapping just over his shoulder.

"Hey, Skylar, you can take the food," Solaria said. "If I wasn't a mover, I'd have dropped things several times on the way here. Just be thankful Nada and I were on our way to the hangar and had to pass the kitchens, or you'd be running over there to get your own breakfast."

Skylar grabbed the polyform box she thrust at him as she came up the ramp. She then took a firmer grip on the other box she had balanced on her opposing hand. "Thanks for getting this. It helps get us in the air that much faster."

"Which is the only reason we did it," Leonada said. "Well, that and we needed breakfast too."

Skylar carried the box toward command as Filzbalm landed on the rim of it and peered down. *What did they bring me? I need breakfast too. It sounds like we're leaving too quickly for me to go fishing.*

"We'll go through it in a second." Skylar turned into the door leading to command. From the smells of the box in his hand it was a good mix of pastries and meats. There were several covered plates in the carton, so he couldn't tell exactly was in there.

"Don't worry, Filzbalm," Solaria said. "You know I'm always going to take good care of you."

Skylar wasn't sure if Filzbalm had included her in his communication, or if she had deduced what he'd said from Skylar's response and knowing the Solar Drake. Either way, it was a sign of how close they all were.

"There you are," Del said from the pilot's chair. "Astara's got the engines warmed up and we're ready to go."

"Main hatch is closed," Astara reported from her normal spot between the pilot and co-pilot's seats.

"Then let's get going." Del tapped his console and the main screen came to life, showing the view from the front of the ship. "We can eat on the way."

"Sounds good." Skylar found the cup of raw meat intended for Filzbalm and put it in the cup holder on the end of the arm of his seat. Before Skylar could get anything out for himself, Filzbalm was perched next to the cup and pulling strips of meat out.

"Thanks for grabbing breakfast, girls," Del said as Astara rose up and moved slowly out the main hangar doors. "Helps get us going faster."

"Sure thing," Solaria said around a mouth full of food. "Anything to get the hunt moving along."

Once clear of the hangar, Astara angled up into the sky. Skylar had to hold onto the box of food to keep from spilling it onto his chest. When she reached altitude and leveled out, he took out a plate and handed it to Del.

Del opened it, frowned, and handed it back. "I bet this one's for you."

Skylar opened the plate he had and found some pieces of thinly sliced fish and some of the sweet rolls that Del liked. "And this one's yours." He handed the plate to Del, taking back the one that was the bran apple muffins he really enjoyed along with a sausage whose ingredients were a mystery to him, but tasted great. Knowing that the kitchen did breakfast buffet style, he glanced back over his shoulder and smiled at Solaria. "Thanks for getting the stuff we like."

Solaria shrugged as she finished chewing the mouth full of food she'd been working on. "Hey, I'm your friend and a predator. I notice all the little things even when I don't point them out."

"And she had me along to fix her mistakes," Leonada added with a chuckle.

"We should be approaching the islands in a few minutes," Astara announced. "My scans show that they are still there, but there is also a large storm currently over the area. It may make landing difficult. There is also a chance we'll be spotted as the clouds will show my passage and the lighting might interfere with my cloaking technology."

Skylar often wondered why nothing ever worked out easily. It would be nice if they could have one adventure without running into problems. "But do you think you can navigate through the storm?"

"I should be able to," Astara replied. "I'm just not sure it'll be undetected."

"At least if it's storming, it'll be cooler," Solaria said.

Skylar wanted to say they'd do it regardless. He wanted to get down on the islands and figure out what the Boarisk were up to, but he wasn't the one in charge. There really wasn't any one of them in charge, unless they wanted to count Astara as in charge since technically she didn't need any of them to be able to operate. The AI armada had functioned just fine for hundreds of years without humans, or humanoids, around to help it out. "What do you guys think? I say we go in and see what we can find."

"I'm always up for a hunt, you all know that," Solaria replied as she crumpled up the box her breakfast has been in. "A little adverse weather just makes it more interesting."

"I'm game," Leonada said.

"Sure." Del didn't sound as positive as the others. It made Skylar wonder if he was worried about somehow damaging Astara with either the landing or the take off. He'd spent so much time working on the ship, it would be a shame to have something happen on their first outing that was more than just a test run or a salvage mission.

"Alright. Plotting course through the storm," Astara said. "I have the cloaking field engaged."

"What if we come in low?" Solaria suggested. "You know, right above the ocean. If we're not passing through the clouds, won't that diminish the chances of us being spotted?"

"Either that or go high and then cut straight down through the clouds," Skylar added around a bite of muffin.

"Low makes sense to me," Del said.

"Low it is then," Astara announced. "We will descend to sea level in five minutes. That should give you plenty of time to finish your morning refueling."

"Breakfast, Astara," Leonada said from her seat behind Skylar. "It's called breakfast. Honestly, Del, you need more work on some of her idiosyncrasies. Even if you can eventually get her humanoid form looking…well…more human, if she talks like that she's going to stand out."

"You make it sound like she'll be leaving the ship at some point," Del said. "We hadn't really planned for that."

"Although it might be interesting," Astara said. "To be able to go places that my ship's body is too large to fit into." She looked over her metallic shoulder toward Leonada. "Perhaps you would be interested in helping me be more human in my conduct. I have noticed that bipedal females tend to be more sensitive to that sort of thing than the males."

"For starters you really shouldn't be using bipedal," Leonada said. "Who says that? Most of us just use humanoid, although when you stop to think about it, that's rather speciesist too."

"It's a Filzbalm word," Skylar said. "Although how she's learning Filzbalm's words, I don't know." The Solar Drake hadn't given any indication that he was speaking to the AI ship, unless he was somehow doing it through Del.

"She hasn't heard it from me." Filzbalm finished off his meat and hurried up to Skylar's shoulder, positioning himself carefully on his pad there.

"I've been monitoring some of the communications between the Tursiops and the Resmordians. The Resmordians use the term all the time," Astara explained. "There are also numerous uses of the word in many of the non-humanoid textbooks I've been downloading in an attempt to bring myself up to speed on the universe. If it isn't an appropriate term, then I shall stop using it."

Skylar hadn't really thought about it. It really was a better term than humanoid, since there were a few bipedal species that weren't humanoid. He'd met an advanced avian boy back at Stars' End. The boy hadn't come to Tursipia with them, but had gone to one of the other temporary campuses. There were also some insectoids who, although they had more limbs, tended to just walk around on two. "I think we're going to need to ponder that."

Del nodded. "I agree. We do know a fair number of non-bipedal people, but humanoid does sound a bit elitist too." He glanced back at Leonada. "What do you say we get back to you on this?"

"That's acceptable," Astara replied. "I don't want to have habits that make people uncomfortable."

"I don't think that's going to be a huge problem," Solaria said. "You've got us around—we're going to make you fit in the best we can."

"Thank you." Astara turned back toward the screen. "We're approaching the edge of the storm. Descending to sea level."

Skylar dropped his plate, empty of everything except the muffin wrapping, into the box, and added Filzbalm's cup once the Solar Drake had licked the blood out of it. Since they were angling down, he knew it wouldn't be safe for him to get up and take the box to the recycling bin, so he waited. Odds were they'd find a safe landing spot and head out quickly, so he could drop it then.

Onscreen, the sky darkened and rain lashed the camera lens, making everything before them fuzzy. Flashes of lightning illuminated the ocean beneath them.

Astara vibrated around them, and the deck rocked back and forth slightly.

"I've never flown through a storm like this before," Astara said. "It is rougher than I anticipated. Trying to stabilize our flight."

"You're doing great," Del said.

No sooner had the words left his mouth, they were pitched to the side. Skylar did his best to hold on to the box with the breakfast garbage in it. Then Astara leveled out.

"Sorry about that." Astara frowned at the main screen. "Some of the updrafts and downdrafts are hard to predict and the lightning appears to be totally random." She lurched again. "I am beginning to believe that Skylar's idea of going in from above the clouds would've been a better option."

Del was bent over his screen. "Looks like we're almost to one of the islands. The larger one. Do you think we can set down there?"

"I believe so," Astara replied. "I am currently scanning for a clear spot large enough for me. We may have to settle for one of the beaches."

"This storm is large enough to be here for a lot longer than we will," Del said glancing up from the screen. "Unless they move the island."

"They are still tethered to the colony on the ocean floor," Astara said. "I do not believe they will be able to terminate that connection quickly."

Del nodded. "Probably not." He moved his hands across the screen. "Looks like the largest unoccupied beach is on the far side of the island. You're going to need to gain some altitude to avoid hitting trees."

"Adjusting flight path," Astara said.

Skylar wished the camera would clear so he could make out more of what they were flying through. It was irritating not being able to see out, and somehow, it felt worse than when they'd first freed Astara and she hadn't had any viewscreen.

She angled upwards, then shook violently before she leveled out.

"What happened?" Solaria asked.

"I was too low and struck a tree," Astara replied. "No major damage. I'll get my nanites on it as soon as we land. Even if it's not repaired, I will still be able to get us back to Aduncus Island."

She lurched to the side again. Skylar didn't adjust the box in time and the garbage inside spilled out. Filzbalm's cup rolled down his front, leaving a trail of bloody dots as it went. He scrambled to try and grab things, but most of it hit the floor as Astara righted herself. Lightning blazed just inches from the camera, causing a blinding flash on the viewscreen.

Forgetting about the remains of breakfast in his lap, Skylar rubbed at his eyes. He blinked several times and his vision slowly returned to normal.

"Del, I think you guys are going to need to find the schematics for some kind of filter for the camera," Solaria said. "Or put it on a delay, so Astara can cut the feed if we're all going to get blinded."

"We're still working out all the kinks—" Del rubbed his own eyes and blinked several times "—we'll get there."

"You are correct, Del, we will get there," Astara said. "We've reached the beach and there is barely room for me to land. I hope my vertical thrusters will be able to fight the winds that are blowing out to sea. This will be a fairly rough landing."

The view out the camera wasn't much better than it had been, but Skylar thought he could make out an expanse of dark beach and the looming shadows of the trees a good distance from the water line. The view kept wobbling as the storm blew Astara around. The violence of the storm was a lot more evident as she hovered there on the vertical thrusters, trying to get them down to the beach. The entire ship shook back and forth as she slowly came out of the sky. The tree line grew more evident, and felt like it was closing in.

Then they dropped several feet and hit with enough force to bounce them all down into their seats, hard. Filzbalm dug into the leather pad on Skylar's shoulder firmly enough for the tips of his talons to prick Skylar's skin.

"We've landed," Astara announced. "I will begin running diagnostics to check for and repair any damage I might have suffered in getting us here."

"Thanks." Del undid his seatbelt. "Let me know if you need me for anything."

Skylar undid his seatbelt and scrambled around to get the garbage that had scattered across the floor. "Let me get this into the recycler and get a clean shirt." He grabbed the last plate, shoved it into the box and stood. "Meet you guys on the ramp."

"You all realize we don't have any rain gear on board," Del said as he stood.

"We'll endure," Solaria said. "Like I said earlier, at least with the storm, it won't be so hot out."

As he headed down the corridor, Skylar wondered how long it was going to be before at least he and Del were going to be colder than they liked while all Solaria and Leonada had to complain about was wet fur. But as long as he was going to be able to find out what was going on, he didn't really care. He wanted to get to the bottom of why the Boarisk were on Tursipia, and make them pay for what they did on Hummassa.

8
Searching the Jungle

AS SOON as they hurried down the ramp, the winds and rain lashed at them. Filzbalm hung on tight to Skylar's shoulder. The way the rain struck Skylar, it felt like ice pricking his face.

"Okay, you guys think we could wait for the storm to pass?" Skylar muttered, although they'd already discussed it on the way down the ramp.

"Nope," Solaria said. "Stay close, though, maybe I can do something to lessen the impact of the storm on us."

There was another blast of wind and rain, then it stopped. Instantly, Skylar didn't feel like he needed to be hunched over, struggling for every step through the deluge.

Solaria grinned. "I recently read the principles of putting up a TK shield to help block wind, water, sand, ice, anything blowing. I hadn't had a chance to practice it yet."

"You might've tried it in the shower," Del suggested. "It's not blowing water, but falling and blowing are very similar."

"Good point. I hadn't thought of that." Solaria walked toward the thick tropical foliage that reminded Skylar a lot of Hummassa. "You guys stay close—the larger I make this shield the harder it will be to maintain."

"Storms don't bother me," Del said. "Well, the winds are somewhat annoying."

Solaria paused a couple of steps into the underbrush. "Which way should we go?"

"If you continue heading to the west, you should come to a cluster of buildings showing on my sensors," Astara said through the coms. "It's eleven structures close together. I can't get readings inside all of them. A couple are heavily shielded. I believe one of the shielded ones contains the top of the shaft going to the habitat on the sea floor."

"Okay," Solaria replied. "Keep us moving in the right direction, and we'll see what we can find." She took off along the general path Astara had indicated, or at least what Skylar hoped was the right way.

Since being on Tursipia, he'd not gotten a firm grasp of the cardinal compass points until he could see the sun. Del explained that although most of his people could navigate without the use of landmarks, sometimes when the islands moved, they shifted in their directional orientation, so it wasn't a good thing to get used to using buildings or trees as planetary landmarks as they would probably change. After his explanation, Skylar stopped trying to figure out which way was which and just went with the flow of things.

It took some effort to navigate through the dense jungle. With Solaria continuing to shield them from the storm, Skylar, Del and Leonada had to struggle to clear the way. Where she could, Leonada moved plants aside with her own mover gift. For the heavier concentrations of obstacles, the three worked together, often having to climb over fallen trees or push through dense underbrush.

"You guys know a blind man could follow our trail back to Astara, don't you?" Solaria said after they'd made it about half a mile.

"If we're lucky, there won't be anyone out in this storm," Leonada replied. "And we're not strong enough to float ourselves up and over all of this."

"I'm just wondering if this is an old island," Del said. "This vegetation doesn't make sense for a newly constructed one."

"But if it's an old island, shouldn't it be registering as existing somewhere?" It didn't make sense to Skylar that the island might be old, but not in the planetary network.

"Not if it was reported as lost in a storm," Del said. "That happens sometimes. An island gets destroyed during a storm and if it sinks in certain parts of the ocean, things are deep and dark enough it's never found again."

"Okay, but how would the Boarisk have access to islands that were lost?" Skylar asked as he helped Leonada move a bundle of vines so Solaria could get through. They were rain-slicked, but had tiny thorns that bit into his fingers. He wished they'd thought ahead and brought gloves and equipment that could've cut through the jungle without a problem.

"Not sure," Del said. "Unless they're working with the Orcan clan. The Orcans would know how to file the correct reports to make it look like an island sank, and then make it disappear. Sounds really complicated, and neither species seem to be the planning types."

"Either way, it would be trouble," Solaria said. "Too many enemies could complicate things. We don't need a lot of people looking for us as we dig up info on this operation."

"Right," Leonada agreed. "We need no eyes on us as we slip in and out of this mess."

"Still hoping the storm gives up plenty of cover," Solaria said.

Something moved as Del took his next step, and he was suddenly whipped up into the air. A loud bell clanged.

"Crap!" Leonada shouted and glanced around.

"Del!" Skylar jumped up as Del shot past him, but he was too slow and Del was yanked up and out of Solaria's protective shield.

"Skylar, Solaria!" Del yelled as he flopped on the cable that held him aloft, about ten feet above them.

"I've got the bell," Leonada said and the bell went quiet, then something thudded to the ground a few feet from them.

Solaria frowned. "I can't believe they're using primitive traps to guard their place."

"Whatever," Skylar said. "It's working, isn't it? We've got to get Del down."

"Del, what's the cable made of?" Solaria asked, calling out in a slightly louder voice than she normally used.

"Just a second." Del twisted and reached up to the cable. The winds blew him around and it took a couple of tries to be able to touch the band around his ankle. "Feels like micro steel to me, but I could be wrong."

Solaria nodded. "Skylar, did you bring your multitool?"

"Sure." Skylar reached into his pocket. Since it came in so handy on most of their adventures, he always had the small box that could become nearly any kind of tool with him at all times. He pulled it out.

"I'll fly it up to him." Filzbalm grabbed the tool from Skylar's hand and flew up into the canopy, toward Del. A gust of wind caught him and blew him several feet to the side. His wings were just a blur as he struggled to reach Del. He ducked as a huge leaf spun toward him.

"Be careful," Skylar said through their link. *"If you can't make it up there, maybe Leonada or Solaria can get it to him."*

"I'm almost there." A level of stress and strain Skylar couldn't remember hearing before filled Filzbalm's mental voice.

"A little farther, Filzbalm," Del said, holding out a hand to him. The wind kept whipping him around, creating a moving target for Filzbalm to aim toward.

Then the Solar Drake grabbed Del's fingers and pulled himself in, quickly latching on to Del's wrist.

Skylar wished he was closer and could see exactly what was going on. He was getting a crook in his neck from staring up at the two of them. Del fiddled with the tool's controls, then a small laser torch appeared in his hand.

"Somebody catch me when I fall," Del said as he contorted himself upward to use the torch on the cable.

"I'm going to have to drop the shield to catch him," Solaria said. "Be ready."

Even if she wasn't able to successfully catch Del, the fall wasn't enough to kill him unless he landed wrong. Nevertheless, Skylar held his breath as Del sliced through the cable holding him up and then dropped toward them. He didn't even fall a couple of feet before he stopped in midair and floated toward the ground. Filzbalm stayed with him the whole way.

They all breathed a sigh of relief when Del was back on the ground and Filzbalm flew over to Skylar's shoulder as Solaria got the shield back up.

"Okay, no more of that," Solaria muttered. "The shield's harder to keep up than I thought. Any more major rescues like this and I'm going to need a stimpatch. I bet we didn't bring any from the medkit, did we?"

"Nope, didn't think about it." Skylar didn't like her suggestion that she'd need a stimulus before long.

"Then we better keep an eye out for more traps. Leonada, you're the best hunter, after me, so you get point." Solaria started off through the jungle again, this time with Leonada leading them.

Several times, Leonada spotted more traps. One was a pit trap where the leaves covering it had partially collapsed due to the storm. There was a swinging log that could've easily taken all of them out, but she warned them of the trip wire as soon as she saw it.

"They're going to a lot of trouble to keep people away from their buildings," Solaria said. "After the shield around the whole island, I really expected more high-tech defenses."

"Astara said when we discovered the islands that the shield was old tech," Del reminded them. "I bet they're trying to save money so they can reap as much profit out of this project as possible."

"Makes sense," Solaria agreed. "At least the old school stuff is easier for us to spot, now that we know what we're looking for."

"You are only ten feet from the first building," Astara announced.

It had been so long since she'd said anything, her voice made Skylar jump.

"I wonder if there'll be fewer traps this close in," Leonada said.

"No clue," Solaria replied. "Don't let up on looking for them."

Skylar peered through the foliage but between the dense greenery and the storm, couldn't see anything that far ahead of them. It was frustrating. Although he'd grown up on a tropical world, the past few months had been spent on more open worlds where his line of sight wasn't easily obscured.

"I hate to, but I'm going to drop the shield," Solaria said. "We might find more if we fan out and keeping the shield going like that will be too hard."

Gritting his teeth against the thought of dealing with the storm up close and person, Skylar nodded. "Okay. Let's do this."

Filzbalm settled tight against Skylar's neck. *"Storms are part of life."*

His statement didn't help much when the shield dropped and wind and rain assaulted them as hard or harder than it had on the beach. Skylar had hoped that maybe the denseness of the jungle would help keep some of it off them, but it didn't. The wind was roaring so loud, it made talking difficult.

Skylar reached out his mind to his friends. *"Okay everyone, I'm going to link us, but try to keep from fully going into a mental gestalt."* He knew it could be done, but hadn't practiced much with it.

"It'll be better than trying to hear the coms," Solaria said. *"Plus, it'll help us be silent as we're stalking around their buildings."*

"Let's hope so," Leonada replied.

Although he was hearing their projected thoughts, and apparently they were all hearing each other, Skylar wasn't picking up on anything deep, or any emotions. He didn't feel like he could suddenly use Solaria's mover gift. *"Okay, Solaria, where to?"*

"Hold on," Del said. *"I'm trying to see if I can reach Astara from this far away. We haven't tried that yet. But she can still help guide us."*

"I'm here," Astara said, sounding far away, and Skylar realized that instead of actually being part of the link he'd set up, they were hearing her through her link with Del.

"The building in front of you is not shielded," Astara advised. *"I am also not picking up any life signs from it. There are some life signs farther into the compound. There are a couple that match descriptions of Boarisk, and several that I can't identify. Their gene profile isn't in my database."*

Since they'd seen a fair number of dots on Astara's scans the previous visit that she hadn't been able to identify, her announcement didn't surprise Skylar.

"I think we should check out every building," Solaria said. *"It might give us a better idea what they're doing here."*

"Okay." Skylar agreed, but he still had visions that were a cross between them looking for the scientists on Armstrong's Ring and searching for survivors in Glacier City on Pantheria. The edge of excitement was blunted by the fear of finding something awful.

With Solaria leading the way, they fanned out in the jungle, then paused just feet from the first building. It was close enough to the treeline that leaves from the massive tree Skylar stood under brushed its roof.

"Astara, are you picking up any kind of electronic surveillance?" Solaria asked.

"There are a number of electronic signatures that I cannot fully identify," Astara responded. *"I know they are not surveillance that I am familiar with, but beyond that, I cannot tell."*

Solaria rubbed her hand over her face and frowned. *"Then we've got to keep our fingers crossed. Nada, if something starts going off, we've got to try to short it out."*

"Understand."

"Skylar, you and Filzbalm are with me. Del, you stick with Nada. If something goes wrong, get back to the ship and bring help. The government might not care about what's out here, but I think your grandfather does."

"We can do that." Del didn't sound as if he liked the plan, but it was what they had.

Solaria pointed at Skylar, then took off around the building at a slow jog.

Following her, Skylar slipped in the mud and scrambled to keep his feet. Going through the jungle, there'd been enough leaves and such on the ground that the mud from the storm wasn't a huge problem, but the trees had been cleared from the compound. It didn't look like anyone had gone to the trouble of planting grass, so the dirt had turned to slick, sticky mud.

"Be quiet, Skylar," Solaria said, and Skylar wasn't sure if she'd seen him almost go down or not.

"We're going to need to go slow," Skylar said.

"Okay," Solaria replied. *"But it'll keep us in the storm longer."*

"Then we stay wet," Skylar muttered, doing his best not to let his frustration about their physical condition bleed through their mental connection.

"I can block it for you," Filzbalm said softly enough Skylar knew the Solar Drake wasn't letting the others know he was talking to Skylar.

Skylar reached up and rubbed Filzbalm's small golden horns, that were just long enough they'd started to curl. It was a silent *thank you* that he didn't have to worry about the others hearing and wondering what he was talking about.

Solaria made it to the building's closest door. It wasn't locked and she slipped in. Skylar followed close behind her. Being out of the storm was great, even if it was in a dark area where he had no idea what was about to happen. His only assurances were that Astara had said it was uninhabited.

"I wish we'd brought palm lights." Solaria felt around in the darkness.

Skylar pulled out his multitool and brought up the flashlight ap. He flipped it on and passed the beam through the darkness. *"It's not much, but it's what we've got unless we can find the light switch."* Crates filled the building with only small walkways between them.

Solaria shook her head. *"No light switch. Too much of a chance of someone noticing and coming to investigate."* She walked over to one of the crates and touched it. *"Poly crate."* She ran her claws around all the edges. *"Sealed tight. If we open one, they'll know someone was here."* She frowned. *"Astara, can you scan the crates and tell us what's in them?"*

"Unfortunately not," Astara replied. *"There is something in the area that is resisting me getting a detailed scan lock."*

"Del, Nada, get in here and let's see if we can find a crate we can open." Solaria said.

"We've only got the one light," Skylar reminded her.

Solaria straightened from where she'd been checking another crate to see if there might be an opening. *"That's going to slow us down."*

The door opened again, and Del and Leonada hurried in, shaking water off as they entered the dry space.

"Then let's see about checking the other buildings. If we're fast enough and don't find anything, we can come back here and do a search," Skylar suggested. "We might be able to find out whatever is in these crates.

"Okay, we go on," Solaria grumbled. "Might as well make the most of this storm. I seem to recall more people around when we buzzed the islands before."

Skylar did too, and as they headed back into the storm, he wondered where the people had gone. Maybe they were all down on the ocean floor, or maybe the Boarisk had detected their flyby and started wrapping up their operation, but the crates said if they were closing up shop, they still had things to get off world. That meant Skylar and his friends had time to figure out what was going on and put a stop to it.

Squaring his shoulders, Skylar followed Solaria back out into the storm as the five of them headed toward the next building, one Astara couldn't scan.

9
Visions Of The Past

AGAIN, SKYLAR and Filzbalm followed Solaria as they sneaked around the buildings looking for something that could tell them what the Boarisk were doing on Tursipia. The second building was very similar to the first, just a lot more crowded.

"They're stockpiling stuff, but is it something that's coming out of the ocean or the sea floor, or is it stuff for the underwater habitat they have down there?" Skylar mused as they slipped out of the second building, heading toward the next one.

"We have very strict rules about what leaves the planet," Del replied, reminding Skylar he still had them all mentally linked so they could talk without fear of being overheard. *"Everything has to go through certain channels."*

"Del," Solaria said. *"These are Boarisk we're dealing with here. They aren't exactly the universe's most upstanding citizens."* She stopped at a corner and peered through the storm-whipped rain.

Skylar couldn't argue with using the storm as cover, but he was getting tired of being wet and cold. If they'd known about the storm beforehand, they could've brought weather-appropriate clothing. They might've still ended up with wet hair, but their clothes wouldn't be plastered to their bodies, making them even colder.

"If they have set up on an old abandoned island that the planetary net doesn't know anything about," Leonada threw in, *"there's a good probability they don't care*

about rules and regulations. They're probably sneaking things off planet during security network updates and such."

"*I'm beginning to wonder why the planetary council couldn't find this place,*" Skylar said. "*I mean sure, Astara says it's shielded, but it's old tech, not new. Shouldn't there be some kind of ripples or something to reveal their hiding place?*"

"*You would think.*" Solaria stopped at the next door and tested it. "*Also, does the shield extend into the water?*"

"*Give me a moment to look into that,*" Astara replied.

"*Door's locked.*" Solaria held out her hand to Skylar. "*Let me see the multitool. I think it's got a lock pick in it.*"

"*Why not just do it with your mind?*" Leonada asked.

Solaria frowned and shook her head as Skylar fished the tool out of his pocket. "*I've never been that good with small, delicate things.*"

Leonada grinned. "*Movers gotta move, but only big stuff. Let me see the lock.*" She eased past Solaria and knelt down so she was looking at the lock. "*Looks fairly basic.*" She put her hands on either side of the lock and stared at it. A brief trickle of her power brushed Skylar through their mental link, then she straightened. "*Yeah, not the latest and greatest tech here. Very bargain basement.*" She opened the door and stepped aside for Solaria to go in just as a soft chime rang out.

They all paused, with Solaria the only one inside the building. "*Crap.*"

"*Since you opened the door, I can now detect three life signs in the building,*" Astara advised them. "*Two are Boarisk, and the other I'm not sure of.*"

"Double crap," Solaria said. *"Can you tell if they heard the chime and are heading this way?"*

"They do not appear to be moving in your direction," Astara continued. *"The chime was caused by a beam you broke when you entered. It is primitive system, and I cannot disable it. I believe it will ring each time you pass through it."*

"You said beam," Del cut in. *"Is it wide or narrow?"*

"Narrow, near the floor."

Solaria bent over and looked near the door frame. *"Ah, here's something. I wonder what happens if I unplug it."* She yanked at something, then held up a small box. After a second the box started screaming with a very loud alarm.

"Okay, that was a bad idea." Skylar reached in and grabbed Solaria by the arm and yanked her out of the doorway. *"Let's get back to the jungle."* He let go of her hand as the four of them ran for the protection the thick foliage of the jungle offered.

"There are multiple lifeforms heading your way from various locations," Astara said.

"Intruders!" a Boarisk shouted in a guttural accent.

"Time to run faster," Skylar said as they made it to the jungle.

Several people yelled from behind them. It sounded like there were a ton of folk coming after them.

They didn't have time to be delicate about their run back to the ship. Skylar felt like a fool as he ran as fast as he could. They should've been better. They shouldn't have been detected.

Filzbalm clung to his shoulder, digging in harder than normal to keep from falling off. The storm continued to lash at them as they ran.

Behind them, the sound of people crashing through the jungle propelled them faster. Skylar didn't like running from the fight, but he also didn't want any of them getting hurt. As much as he wanted to disable the Boarisk operation, he knew they needed more knowledge, and hoped they hadn't shown their hand by tripping the alarm the way they had.

"Slow down," Leonada panted through their link. *"I can't run like this right now. We've got some space. I don't hear them anymore."*

Solaria stopped as Skylar did. She spun around and stared back. *"Nada. Oh, geez. I'm sorry, I wasn't thinking."*

Leonada had slowed to a fast walk, or at least as fast as she could considering the thick vegetation. *"I understand. The hunt's gone bad. We get caught up with suddenly being the prey and we just react. No problem."* She stopped and put her hands on her knees. *"I don't like being the weak link in this pursuit."*

"You have all covered half the distance in under half the time," Astara reported. *"You are easily outdistancing your pursuers, although they have not broken off the chase yet."*

Solaria took Leonada's hand. *"Come on Nada, we've got to keep moving, but we can slow down. Astara will let us know if they get too close."*

"That is correct," Astara said.

"I'm going to run ahead and get everything ready for a quick take off," Del said, and vanished into the underbrush.

"We're going to be fine," Solaria said as she started Leonada forward again. *"We've only got a little farther to go."*

Skylar fell in behind them. He wanted to keep running with Del, but felt better staying with Solaria and Leonada. *"I'll watch our backs, in case something slips past Astara."* He knew it was doubtful—with everything Del and Melody had put into the AI ship, she'd spot just about anything that came up on them. But it gave him and Filzbalm something to do.

They made it to a path that ran toward the beach; they hadn't spotted it on their trek to the compound, but it made sense that there would be a path running between the two. When they reached the beach, though, Solaria stopped. The storm seemed to be lessening but she looked a little confused.

"What's wrong?" Skylar asked. Even though he wasn't worried about being overheard, it was easier to be heard mentally over the wind that was still whipping around. Just because it wasn't as strong as it had been earlier didn't necessarily mean it was calm.

"We came out at a different spot than we went in," Solaria replied, still scanning up and down the beach. *"I'm not exactly sure where we parked. The storm's not helping with that."*

"Go to your left," Astara said. *"Follow the curve of the island for about a quarter of a mile. You might want to move a little faster, your pursuit is getting closer."*

Solaria glanced at Leonada. *"Nada, can you move a little faster?"*

Leonada nodded. *"Almost got my wind back."*

Even with the faster pace, Skylar stayed back, making sure to keep himself between Leonada and anyone who might be following them.

"I'm watching," Filzbalm said. *"The rain's letting up, so it's easier to see now."*

"Thanks," Skylar and Solaria said at the same time. It created an odd echo in Skylar's head and he wondered if everyone else felt the same sensation.

"They've cleared the trees," Astara said. *"You'll reach me easily before they can reach you. Just don't slow down."*

Something splashed in the water. Skylar wondered if it was one of their pursuers, or something else.

"Guys, you might want to hurry a little faster," Del said. *"It looks like there four Orcans swimming along the beach, heading toward you."*

"I guess this proves the Orcans are working with the Boarisk," Solaria said. *"Del, Astara, one of you turn off the transceiver. We don't need Astara broadcasting her identifier. Don't want to make their hunt for us too easy."*

"Already done," Astara said. *"Del thought of that a few seconds ago."*

Skylar's breath was coming harder as he raced along the beach. He wanted to get to Astara and back into the sky. He didn't want anything to happen to him or his friends, and if they were captured by either the Orcans or the Boarisk the odds wouldn't be in their favor.

Skylar spotted their original trail through the jungle just as a lance of pain shot through his head. He stumbled and the link he had with his friends dissolved.

"They've got a reader with them!" he shouted as he tried to raise a protective shield around his thoughts. He was their strongest reader. It was his job to protect himself and the rest of them.

"I'm with you," Filzbalm said as Skylar's shield flared to greater intensity.

Another attack made Skylar stumble again—he almost hit the sand as he continued to run toward Astara. He wanted to send a bolt of mental power back at the Orcan, but couldn't do it while running. It was all he could manage, with Filzbalm's help, to keep up the shield that he was trying to extend around himself and the others. If he were to go on the attack, he'd have to stop.

"They're on the beach," Filzbalm said. *"Man, are they big."*

"That's not helping," Skylar didn't want to run past Leonada, so he kept his pace about the same as hers, and she seemed to be lagging.

Del appeared on the beach—obviously, Astara still had her cloaking field up. "Over here."

In the lead, Solaria changed her course slightly with Leonada right behind her.

A bolt from Astara's laser hit the sand behind Skylar. It kicked mud and water around him.

"They're right behind us," Filzbalm said. *"But Astara's lasers are a good deterrent. They're slowing down."*

Solaria and Leonada ran past Del and vanished.

"Get up the ramp!" Skylar shouted, hoping Del would get himself to safety.

Del seemed to wait forever, then took two steps backward and disappeared as Skylar rushed the spot where he'd been. Skylar's feet hit the ramp and it began to close.

There was a little shifting as Astara lifted off the beach.

"Don't go too far." Skylar huffed as he grabbed a rail at the top of the ramp for balance. "I want to get a look at these people."

"Good idea," Del agreed. "Let's get up to command."

Skylar followed Del past the main galley where Solaria was getting Leonada something to drink. When they reached command, Skylar took his seat quickly.

"Astara, I want to see the people who were pursuing us." Skylar buckled himself in as he spoke.

"Of course." The image on the main screen split. It showed four Orcans standing in the surf. They were huge, nearly twice the size of the Orcan Skylar had seen at the Galaxeria. The black and white Tursipians looked furious. On the other screen two Boarisk brandished weapons in the air and shouted while three others stared at the spot where Astara had been moments before.

Skylar's breath caught. One of the men below on the beach had deep red skin, green hair, and three fingers. It was a Hummassan, like Skylar's long-lost friend Teir. He had no idea how a Hummassan had ended up on Tursipia, unless he was one of the ones who had vanished in the same Boarisk attack that killed Skylar's mother. He gripped the arms of his chair hard enough it made his hands hurt. He had to get back down there and find out what was going on. If the Hummassan he was staring down at was part of that attack, he might know what happened to Teir. It was the closest thing Skylar had ever had to a lead, and he didn't want to lose it.

10
Family Party

SKYLAR STUDIED the screen in his cabin on Astara. They hadn't gotten much information on their jaunt to the islands, but there had been a little bit. First and foremost was that there was at least one Hummassan there. He'd been analyzing the many images Astara had taken, and although it wasn't anyone he recognized, he was sure the red-skinned person he'd seen was a Hummassan. The species wasn't prone to space travel—most of them preferred to stay on their home planet. It hadn't taken Skylar much effort to learn there weren't any other known species that matched the general description of the Hummassans. Just to be sure, Skylar had Del double-check his findings.

It was all Skylar could do to not go rushing back to the islands, find the red-skinned man, and save him from the Boarisk. Unfortunately, Professor Aduncus had requested, or ordered depending on who was talking at the time, that they stay on Aduncus Island until their next free day, which was five days from their adventure in the storm. Solaria figured it was to prevent them from getting into trouble, and Del suspected his grandfather had taken the information and gone back to the council to attempt to get them to do something about the Boarisk living on Tursipia. Since they'd gotten back, the professor was more shielded than normal and none of them wanted to be rude enough to probe him to find out what was going on. Regardless of the real reason, Skylar was impatient to be out there and finding answers.

Del stuck his head into Skylar's open cabin door. "Hey, Skylar."

Skylar tapped off his screen and turned to face Del. "What's up?"

"Grandfather asked me to find you and ask that you make it to dinner tonight." Del leaned against the door frame. "It's not in the cafeteria, but at the main family house."

"What's going on?" Skylar glanced at the time on his com. It wasn't long before everyone normally ate.

"Squeela's birthday." Del rolled his eyes. "She's making a huge fuss over turning fifteen and ask for me to bring all my friends. Grandfather agreed that it was probably a good idea."

"I'm even invited," Astara said, joining Del. "I've been working on moving my drone body farther from the ship, so there shouldn't be any problem."

"Sounds like fun," Skylar said. He hadn't had a ton of time with Del's family since he'd been on the island. He'd spent most of his days either in classes or doing training exercises. Although he'd been an only child and his birthdays were normally just him and his mother going to do something, like a night out for dinner and a visit to the local arcade, he'd spent a few birthdays with Teir and his large family. Those times had always been enjoyable, and made Skylar wonder what life would've been like if he'd had brothers and sisters, even though he knew that was unlikely in most of the Galactic Council-controlled space. Except on sparsely populated planets like Tursipia, families were limited to one child, occasionally two if something happened to the first one early in life.

"I'm coming too." Filzbalm flew from his perch platform above the foot of Skylar's bed and landed on Skylar's shoulder.

"Solaria and Leonada said they'd meet us there," Del said as he straightened form the door frame. "Don't worry about changing. In case you haven't noticed, we're a fairly laid-back family. What you've got on is going to be fine."

Skylar chuckled as he stood from his desk chair. "Thanks. That's one of the things I like about your family, how mellow you all are. I'm not sure if it's from being part dolphin, or something else."

Del frowned as they started down the corridor to the ramp. "You know, I think as we find out more about the species that are mergers of humans and other lifeforms, we're going to discover stuff like that. The things that help define us as a people are some of the same parts of ourselves that help set us apart from humans. I can think of several examples."

"Like Pantherians and their need to hunt?" Skylar suggested. Since they'd had confirmation of humans using illegal gene-splicing technology to make a number of the species that people throughout the galaxy thought of as original species, he'd stopped from time to time and thought about the species he knew for sure were manipulated. There were only a couple he'd had much contact with, Pantherians and Tursiops being the ones he was most familiar with. He could see Solaria's primal need to hunt and kill as part of the descriptions of the big cats of Sol Three. She'd gotten more than just her furry appearance from her feline ancestors. The Tursiops were overly smart and gregarious, much like their dolphin progenitors.

"Exactly," Del agreed as they started down the ramp. "I really think there's a lot more we need to research on all this. Even with what Astara had from the AI network, there's still holes in our knowledge. Some of the original species show evidence of having been on their planets since before the stargate network was a thing. There's got to be other factors we don't know about."

Skylar shrugged. He had so much on his mind, he hadn't given much thought to places where there were holes in theories. "Maybe time travel?"

Del shook his head. "Time travel only exists in cheap science fiction stories and old serialized vids. It's not a real thing. There's no way to go fast enough to go forward in time and you can't stop time and throw everything in reverse to go into the past. I think if it were possible, we'd have done it by now."

"Probably." Sad that there wasn't time travel in their reality.

"Over the course of our journeys from the Sol system, we encountered several anomilies that might have led to time travel," Astara said. "Perhaps it is something we can investigate at a later time."

"That would be good," Skylar said. He liked the idea there was new things in the universe they might be able to discover and explore.

"Yes, it would," Del agreed. "But we need to focus on the here and now, and between our adventures and working on continued mods in your design and programming, I'm starting to fall behind in school."

"What?" Skylar hadn't had any clue that was happening. If there was anyone he never expected to fall behind in studies, it was Del. He seemed to thrive on learning new things. "That's not possible."

Del chuckled. "Even my brain gets tired after a while. Right now, Galactic History and Universal Literature don't hold much interest. Astara is so full of practical new ideas and info that I haven't stopped to think about some of my classes. I need to fix that, or Grandfather's going to get upset."

"That might be an understatement." Although Skylar had rarely known Professor Aduncus to even raise his voice, the idea of Del failing classes might be a straw that caused him to snap. He was taking being in charge of the students on Tursipia fairly seriously.

"The next few weeks or so, I want you to make sure I'm doing my studying and not just getting all wrapped up in mods and stuff," Del said as they walked across the hangar toward the big open doors leading onto the beach.

"If either of you give me the ideas I need to implement, I'm sure I can handle most of my mods myself," Astara said. If she'd been more emotional, Skylar was fairly sure there would've been a tinge of irritation in her normally even voice.

"I'm sure you can," Del said, patting her on the shoulder.

"I don't have a problem keeping you both on track," Skylar said. "Maybe you can help me with some of my studies too. I'm working with Solaria on trying to sort out some of the galactic past that the corps are covering up. Perhaps some of the classes you're struggling with might give us more holes to chase down and find the answers for."

Del laughed. "More holes to chase down? Now you're sounding like Solaria and Leonada. You need to start spending more time with non-predatory races. Or at least folks who don't spend all their free time thinking about hunting."

"There's nothing wrong with thinking about hunting," Filzbalm said. *"Some of those hunting ideas might be exactly what we need for dealing with the Boarisk on the islands."*

"You both have good points," Skylar said as they started across the sand toward the main house.

Del frowned. "Is Filzbalm countering my hunting comments?"

Skylar shrugged as they entered the shade of one of the largest trees on the island. "Sorta. But he's right—

we're going to need hunting skills to deal with the Boarisk."

"Don't have a counter for that one," Del agreed. "I still can't believe the planetary council is having such an issue with taking action even though they're having dificulty finding the island."

"I think we're all learning that the government and the corps aren't very useful for a lot of things." As they slipped out from the tree's shade, Skylar enjoyed the sun on his face for a couple of minutes as they finished the trip to the house. "That's why groups like Intragal Rescue are so important. They help fill the gaps where the government and corps fail."

"Yeah, it's too bad we can't call Phil with our findings and have him declare a humanitarian emergency and get some help down here." Del held the door open for Skylar.

"That's something I hadn't thought about. Maybe we need to call him and ask." Skylar skidded to a stop and stared. He'd been in the main house a few other times, but never for an event like a birthday party.

Someone had taken the time to decorate the main hall of the building. There were bright streamers stretched around the room. Several holograms lit up the far end of the hall near the head of the table. One of them said "Happy 15th Squeela!" in bright blue and yellow text. Two others in the corners had a dolphin jumping out of the surf. A fourth was a bright unicorn with a rainbow mane and tail running back and forth between the dolphins.

From the number of people already there, Del, Skylar, Filzbalm, and Astara were the last to arrive.

"About time you guys got here," Click, Del's brother, said. He looked a lot like Del and their grandfather, with smooth dark gray skin and, like Del, short dark hair.

"Sorry, we had farther to come," Del said.

The response made Skylar wonder if there was something going on between the two of them. The Aduncus family were all mid to strong level psychics, all except for Del, and Skylar often felt sad for his friend when they were around more of his family than Professor Aduncus. They didn't mistreat him…exactly, but they were sometimes short and snarky with him in ways that made Skylar uncomfortable. He'd heard tales from Del, Solaria, and some of the other students that in a psychic society someone's ranking on the psychic talent scale influenced the way others behaved around them. Del was a level two feeler, fairly low on the scale of what was considered the weakest of the three acknowledged gifts. Since his ability to bond with mechanical intelligences or AIs like Astara was a new skill, people weren't sure how to react. His family, at least, continued dealing with him like they always had, somewhat more distantly than they treated their stronger members.

"Del, Skylar!" Squeela hollered and dashed toward them. She was wearing a short sparkling dress and her long, light blue hair flowed out behind her.

She caught Del in a hug, then grabbed hold of Skylar. Even with Solaria's observations about how some of Del's family were more than a little interested in the new students living on their island, he hadn't done anything to encourage Squeela's interest in him. He made sure to not do anything to make her think he was interested, and even kept his mental shields low when she was around, hoping she'd pick up on things on her own. She was a mid-level feeler, so unless she was just being incredibly dense, that should've done the trick.

"Thanks for coming, Skylar," she whispered in his ear as her hug lasted a little longer than Skylar was comfortable with. "You too, Filzbalm."

"Del said it was your birthday," Skylar said. "Thanks for inviting us. If he'd told us ahead of time, I would've found something to bring." Since she included Filzbalm in her greeting, Skylar used *us*. Most people in Del's family had gotten used to that as Skylar's way of reminding people Filzbalm was as sentient as any of them.

Squeela hooked her arm through Skylar's and then Del's. "Just you being here is present enough for me." She led them toward the head table, where Del's parents and grandparents tended to eat. Normally Del and Skylar, the couple of times they had come to the main house for meals, had eaten with Del's other cousins and his brother on the lower tables.

"Looks like everyone made it," Del said.

"Of course they did." Squeela laughed. "It's a party."

Del's father came over to them. "Del, your grandfather has something he wants to discuss with you and Skylar after the celebration. I told him we weren't going to interrupt the festivities."

Del nodded. "Thanks for letting me know, Dad."

The announcement sent a thrill of excitement through Skylar. He hoped that the planetary council had decided to do something on the three islands. He figured anything else would be aimed at more than just Del and Skylar, unless Solaria's Uncle Phil had discovered something useful about finding Teir and had sent the professor a message to pass along. He wanted to go find Professor Aduncus and get the message, but he'd learned how Del's family handled things like family parties and if the professor had said it could wait, it could.

Squeela pouted as Del's father walked away. "This is my party, Del."

Del patted her arm. "We all know that, Squeela, that's why we're waiting until after the party to talk about whatever it is Grandfather wants to talk about."

She stuck her lip a little farther out. "And see that you keep it that way." She glared at Del. "Do I make myself clear?"

Skylar smiled. "Don't worry Squeela, I'll make sure you have a happy birthday." As soon as he said it, he mentally kicked himself. He'd been doing such a good job about not saying or doing anything to lead her on, then he put his foot in it.

She grinned wildly. "When you're around, it's always a happy day, Skylar."

"You know, I really don't understand any of this mating stuff," Filzbalm said. *"Is it really necessary to be so awkward around her?"*

"There is no mating crap, and you know it," Skylar said, hoping Professor Aduncus, or Solaria wasn't close by and listening in. *"I'm just trying to be nice."*

"I don't think she is," Filzbalm said. *"I think she's got her sights set on you. Are you really that good of a catch?"*

Squeela patted Skylar's arm. "You know it's not nice to be mentally speaking to someone else when you've got a pretty girl on your arm. No offense, Filzbalm."

"Sorry. Filzbalm was just wondering if I thought if either your mom or Del's had remembered to set out some raw meat for him. He's gotten particularly fond of fresh fish." Skylar hoped she wasn't sensitive enough to pick up on his lie.

"That's not what we were talking about," Filzbalm said.

"But she doesn't need to know what we were talking about," Skylar replied.

"I'm sure somebody thought about him," Squeela said, then looked onto Skylar's shoulder where Filzbalm perched. "I think the entire family loves having you around, Filzbalm. Everyone is always talking about you, saying nice things even."

"That's nice of them," Filzbalm said and stretched across the distance from Skylar's shoulder to Squeela's.

"Thanks, he appreciats that." Skylar relayed.

When they reached the table, Solaria and Leonada were already there, sitting off to one end. They had their heads bowed in hushed conversation, if such a thing was really possible in a room full of psychics, some of whom were strong readers. Down the table from them, toward the opposite end, were a few of Del's other younger cousins.

"Okay, Skylar, you sit here beside me." Squeela pointed to the seat just to her left. "Del, you're between him and Leonada."

"Thanks," Skylar said, really wishing he could swap places with Del. "What about Astara?"

Squeela looked confused, then glanced next to Del where Astara's drone body stood. "Oh, I didn't think she eats. I figured she could just stand around somewhere."

"I can find a spot to be out of the way," Astara replied. "I do appreciate your invitation. I've been wanting to observe more humanoid rituals."

"It's a birthday party," Squeela said, looking indignant. "It's not a ritual."

"In many ways it is," Del said. "We just don't stop to think of things like birthday parties as ritualized."

"Del, don't go getting all Mr. Smartypants on me right now." Squeela seemed a lot older than fifteen. "Tonight is my night. You can get superior on *your* birthday. Do you understand me?" There was a no-nonsense edge to her tone, and Skylar suddenly realized that Squeela might be nearly a year younger than he was, so she wasn't just a silly little girl, but quickly becoming a force to be reckoned with.

Kreela, Del's aunt and Squeela's mother appeared, carrying a tray of baked fish. The smell made Skylar's mouth water. He hadn't realized how hungry he was until the aroma of the food hit him. It was some of the best-smelling food he'd been around in a long time.

He waited until Squeela took her seat, then sat. Filzbalm hopped from her chair over to his as the meal began. For the next hour, everyone took turns getting up and walking over to praise Squeela for becoming a lovely young woman. After the main course, there were small pastries brought out, served with an ice treat that Skylar didn't have a name for. It was shaved ice with fruit chunks and flavored syrup poured over it's surface.

When everyone was finished eating, people brought Squeela presents. Several of the young men from the surrounding islands paid homage to her, casting Skylar harsh glances. He ignored them and focused on having fun with a family. It was something he'd never expected to do again, after his mother died. It felt great. The time on Pantheria with Solaria's family had been quieter and more intimate, but Del's big family was doing a great job of making Skylar feel welcome.

11
Receiving Permission

SKYLAR STRECHED and yawned. Above him, on his platform, Filzbalm did the same.

"Breakfast would be good," the Solar Drake said.

"Yeah it would," Skylar agreed. He glanced up at the clock on the shelf near Filzbalm's platform. They had just enough time for a quick shower and something from Astara's galley, or to skip a shower and make it to the campus kitchen for breakfast with everyone else.

"If you're going to get a shower, I think I'm going to fly over to the kitchen. Astara's regenerated meat isn't the same as fresh fish." Filzbalm shook himself and spread his bright orange wings.

Skylar yawned again and got out of bed. "Sounds like a good idea. I'll catch you later."

Filzbalm flew from his platform toward the small opening above the main door. It was a spot Del had Astara create for him, once they'd decided which cabin was going to be Skylar's. *"If I hurry, I'll have time for a quick swim before class,"* he said. Then Filzbalm was gone.

One of the nice things about being on Tursipia was how Del's family treated Filzbalm like all the other students. On Star's End, he had been Skylar's pet more than mental bond partner. Here, Del's mother, or one of his many cousins helping out with meals, would get Filzbalm a fresh fish as soon as he appeared on the counter of the kitchen near the other kids wanting food.

Skylar grabbed his towel and bathroom kit and headed toward the bathroom that served all of Astara's cabins. He didn't mind sharing, and at least it was just him and Del and not all the other kids like it had been before they'd been given permission to move out of the dorm and onto the ship.

Del's cabin door opened and Fin, one of their roommates from Stars' End, walked out. "I'll catch you later." His blue hair was slightly disheveled and his shirt wasn't tucked all the way in.

Skylar didn't hear what Del's reply was.

"Hey, Skylar," Fin said on his way past.

Skylar gave Fin a short nod, not exactly sure what to say. "Hey, Fin."

He stood there for a second with his hand on the bathroom door as Fin headed down the hall and out of Astara. One of the first things Skylar had learned about being a psychic was that it was impolite to go digging around in other people's minds, or even their emotions. That was why shielding was so important. After his little talk with Solaria on the beach, he was passingly curious about what was going on between his two friends, but figured that if Del wanted him to know, he'd say something.

With a sigh, Skylar went on to the bathroom for his shower.

"I SHOULD'VE warned you about Fin," Del said later as he got a breakfast bar from the food generator.

Skylar shrugged as he finished up his protein patty and toast with fruit jell. "What was there to warn me about?"

Del walked over to the table where Skylar sat and plopped down in the chair opposite of him. "That we're playing around." It was Del's turn to shrug. "Look, I've never picked up any kind of…ah…sexual feelings from you one way or that other. That's kind of odd for Tursiops—we really enjoy being close to one another, and I thought most humans did too."

"Not something I've put much thought into," Skylar said. "Before I bonded to Filzbalm, I didn't really care one way or the other, and…" He paused searching for the right words. "Honestly, now I couldn't care less. There's so much going on, and I've never really stopped and thought about having kids, or having someone around all the time. Getting used to being able to join minds with other people and with Filzbalm is still a little odd for me. I really can't imagine being physically close to anyone. If you and Fin are exploring things, that's great. Have fun. I'm going to stick in my cabin and play games when we're not out doing other stuff."

Del smiled. "Thanks. I wasn't sure how you were going to deal with that. We Tursiops are open about things like that, but I know a lot of the other species can have hangups. I don't think Pantherians would. They're just as open about natural life…things as we are, but I've heard some races, like the Boarisk, are very masculine-driven." He paused and chewed his breakfast bar. "Okay, I don't know if that's the right word or not."

Skylar laughed. "That's okay. I totally understand what you're trying to say. Sort of like my mom was about psychics, but in relation to other things. Got it. No worries. Hummassans were very open about things like that too. Nothing new to me, although Fin in the hallway did take me by surprise."

"I'm glad we're good. Things with Fin are interesting, but I feel there's something lacking. I don't know." Del chewed some more and put his elbows on the table. "But then Tursiops often have large households, so maybe that's part of what's missing."

"Don't look at me for that." Skylar held up a hand. "Like I said, not interested."

Del nodded. "Wasn't suggesting, just mulling things over in my head." Then he grinned. "But it's nice being able to talk to you about it. Life is easier with friends to bounce ideas and thoughts off of."

Although Skylar wasn't sure he was totally at ease talking about emotional stuff with anyone, he'd bear through it for Del and Solaria. They were his best friends and even if the subject matter didn't interest him, he could still listen to them. Sometimes listening was what friends did best.

Skylar's com chimed with his warning alarm to get to class. "Come on." He grabbed his plate and tossed it toward the recycling module. "We need to get." His plate missed the module and clanged to the floor. "You know, sometimes I think it would be good to be a mover. I'd never miss tossing something into recycling." He dashed over and put the plate in.

"Yeah, there are definite advantages to Solaria's power set," Del agreed as he stood and headed toward the door. "But you know, I don't think I would change things now." He paused in the doorway and put a hand on the threshold. "I like being able to talk with Astara. It might get a little loud if there were other AIs around, but she's it at the moment, and I'm good with that."

"Thank you, Del," Astara said as she walked down the hall toward them. "I'm good with you being able to talk to me too. I guess we need to get to class."

Del nodded. "That we do."

Skylar walked along with them as the three of them headed out. At first he'd thought it was odd that Professor Aduncus had wanted Astara to attend classes with them, but then he realized the Professor was treating her like any other sentient. He obviously felt she could learn from being with other people and might even pick up a few things from a classroom setting. It might not have been such a smooth transition if they'd still been on

Stars' End and under the stricter regulations there, but on Aduncus Island, things were rather laid-back and mellow.

"MR. MARS, if you would please close the door," Professor Aduncus asked as Skylar hurried into his office. The first thing that hit Skylar was that he and his friends were in trouble. Solaria, Del, Leonada, Astara and Del's brother Click were all there.

Seeing Click was a surprise. He hadn't been around much since Skylar had been on the island.

Skylar closed the door and then walked over to take the only empty chair in front of the professor's desk. After he sat, Filzbalm unwrapped his tail from around Skylar's neck and shoulders, flew over to Leonada's chair, and rested his head on her shoulder.

"What are you doing?" Skylar asked. Since their close call on the island with the Boarisk, Filzbalm was closer to Leonada than before, and Skylar had been too busy to ask him about it.

"Listening for her baby," Filzbalm replied. *"I can sense its emotions, and there have been a couple of thoughts. It's interesting. I know Solar Drakes start picking up things when we are still in our eggs. Her baby isn't inside an egg, exactly, but as it grows bigger it's starting to be more aware of..."*

Professor Aduncus cleared his throat. "Mr. Mars, Filzbalm."

"Oh. Sorry, sir." Skylar stopped chatting with his bond mate and focused on the professor.

"You both know it's rude to do that in a room with other readers. Do you mind telling us what is so important as to delay our conversation?"

Skylar glanced at Filzbalm and then back at the professor. "Filzbalm is hoping to hear Leonada's baby again."

Leonada glanced at Filzbalm, then put her hand on her stomach. "Again? I haven't picked up anything more than basic emotions from him. You've heard him thinking?"

Filzbalm nodded. *"Not in words, just pictures. He doesn't like being jostled around when you run. It makes him queasy."*

Skylar chuckled and relayed what Filzbalm said.

"I doubt I'm going to get out of physical activity just because the baby doesn't like it," Leonada said, then grinned at her stomach. "I wish I was a reader so I could communicate with him as soon as possible."

"I doubt that, Ms. Cloudara." Professor Aduncus steepled his fingers and rested his elbows on the desk. "From my understanding, most readers have harder than normal pregnancies due to the demands of having a link with their child that's impossible to block out until they leave the womb. It's much like the bond Mr. Mars and Filzbalm have, but with a less cognitive partner. You'll find motherhood challenging enough without having your child's wants and needs constantly in your head. And no, you don't get to get out of physical activity unless it's determined that it is causing your child harm, and that's not my decision to make. Now, let's get on to why I called you all together."

Skylar reached over and offered Filzbalm his hand so the Solar Drake would be more focused sitting with him. Filzbalm stepped over, then scampered up to Skylar's shoulder.

"As you all know, I've been relaying the information that you've found about the island of Boarisk here on Tursipia. At this time, the ruling council can't find any evidence of the island and they refuse to believe it exists, even with the images you brought back. They are currently comparing the images with the tree configuration of all registered islands."

"But they aren't going to find anything," Del said. "There's aren't currently any missing islands, and that means this one is either new, or one that was reported sunk in a storm. Due to the trees, I'm willing to bet it was lost in a storm."

Professor Aduncus sighed and stared at Del. "And if you wouldn't be so eager about things, I'll finish my thought. Del, please realize that just because you're my grandson doesn't mean you can appear to have special privileges when there are other students around, at least outside of the people gathered in this room." For a moment an uneasy silence filled the office, then the professor continued. "I believe you. Even without scanning your minds about the incident, none of you are prone to making up things. Please realize that if I didn't trust you all, Astara would be confined to the island."

Del paled slightly and bowed. "Thank you, Grandfather."

"Just don't make me regret that trust. So, since the council members are being sticks in the mud, and I don't like the idea of Boarisk on our planet, we need to do something about it. First we need to figure out what they are doing here. To that end, I want you to take Click and at least two other young people with you, preferably movers. Go back to the island. Get your hands on one of those crates and bring it back so we can find a way to open it and see what's inside. Be careful, since Boarisk aren't susceptible to telepathic influence. Where you might be able to cloud the minds of other species, it won't work with them."

Skylar's heart pounded fast. They were getting permission to see what was going on. It was not a combat mission, just recon, but it was a move against the Boarisk.

"Since Astara has stealth technology now, thanks to Del helping her incorporate modern advancements, I want her to take you back to the island." The professor's gaze landed on Astara. "That is… if you don't mind going on the mission."

Astara shook her head. "If Del is going, I need to be there to help protect him."

Click laughed. "You've already got the girls trying to protect you, Del. In a few years, entire pods will be following you around."

Del glared at his brother, but didn't say anything.

"Thank you, Astara," Professor Aduncus said. "Now, Click, you work with Solaria and Astara on a plan. Take the next two days to do it. If you disappear during off days, there's less chance of the other students talking about it. I might even authorize a trip to the Galaxeria if I can arrange transport." He looked at Skylar, Del, and Solaria. "Since the last school transport was destroyed before the AI armada attack, anything that involves more than a couple of students at a time has been harder to organize. I'll contact Ms. Grissom and see what we can do."

"It might not be a good idea to tell her what we're up to," Skylar said, then instantly hit himself for suggesting that he keep something from her. Part of reader society was not keeping secrets or lying.

"Sometimes it is better to ask forgiveness than permission." Professor Aduncus gave Skylar a slight grin. "None of us really think of you all as children anymore, not after everything you've been through in the past months. You've proven yourselves reliable and resourceful. Should something go wrong, and do everything you can to make sure it doesn't, I will handle Ms. Grissom."

"Thank you, Professor," Solaria said as she looked at Click. "How soon do we need to start planning? I love planning hunts."

"After dinner tonight would be soon enough," Click said.

"Very good." Professor Aduncus stood. "Then all of you head off to dinner and we'll get together to go over the plan before you leave."

Skylar rose and left the room with his friends. He couldn't believe Professor Aduncus was giving them clearance to head back to the island, even if it was just supposed to be recon. It was great being treated like an adult. Ever since their battle on Pantheria, everyone associated with the school had stopped treating him and the others like kids.

He knew if his mother was still alive, none of it would be happening. But as much as he missed her, he wouldn't change the feeling that he had a handle on his destiny.

12
Under the Cover of Darkness

SKYLAR HELD on as Astara banked hard and dove out of the night sky toward the cloaked island.

"Coming in low is probably a good idea," Click said from the co-pilot's chair.

Although it made sense for the older Aduncus brother to sit there, Skylar felt very strange not sitting in his regular seat and being consigned to the back row next to Solaria. Leonada was in the rear with two Tursiops who Skylar didn't know. They were friends of Click's who had been selected for the mission based on their battle prowess in some of the ritual games most young Tursiops engaged in. Those weren't one of the things Del enjoyed, so he hadn't had a lot to say about them. He also didn't know the two very well, and couldn't tell Skylar and the others anything interesting.

"Right, we've gone over that," Del muttered as Astara leveled out just above the waves. He'd been quiet and touchy since their grandfather had suggested Click go with them and help ensure everyone got home safely.

"Cloak is engaged," Astara said from her normal spot between the two front seats. "We'll make it through the island's shield in thirty seconds."

"Go in slow," Click said. "You know, it feels strange telling the ship what to do as opposed to actually flying it myself."

"That's the advanced technology we have access to," Del said. "When you show computers how to think for themselves, they don't need us to be so hands on."

"At least she's not trying to kill us," Click muttered. He'd been with them during the battle with the AI armada, but hadn't had much to do with Astara since they'd all come to Tursipia.

"Thankfully, Del was able to override my base programming," Astara said. "We are through the shield."

Click leaned forward, eyes wide. "There really is an island here. I read over the reports, both yours and the council's, but I wasn't totally convinced. I'd love to know how they are not getting detected by the planetary satellites."

"I would too," Del said. "It doesn't make sense that Astara can see through their sensors and nothing else can."

"Right." Click settled back in his seat.

Although Skylar wasn't totally sure how the planetary sensor array worked, he figured the Boarisk were either paying someone off to look the other way or had someone on the inside who was making sure the existence of the islands stayed hidden. He and Del had sat up with Solaria for a couple of nights discussing it, and that was the only plausible idea they had. Apparently Del hadn't shared that with Click.

"The same beach we landed on last time?" Astara asked as the approached land.

"That's the plan," Del said. "It's fairly close to their buildings, and without the storm pounding away on us, we shouldn't have as much of a fight getting there."

Astara slowed and then hovered a second before she lowered herself to the beach. Fine sand blew up, causing strange patterns in the soft landing lights, then stopped. For just a moment, the effect reminded Skylar some of the snow on Pantheria.

Click unbuckled his seatbelt and stood. "Alright folks, everyone stick with your partners. If something happens, get back to the ship. Astara, be ready to shoot anyone who isn't us."

"I will do so," Astara said.

Skylar, with Filzbalm on his shoulder, stood and went to the back of the ship where everyone else was gathered at the opening for the ramp.

Filzbalm and Gal, the biggest of the two guys who'd come with Click were Skylar's team. Gal was a huge Tursiops—he reminded Skylar of the Orcan at the Galaxeria, even if his coloring was Tursiops, dark gray with short blue hair. They were to go north and stick to the beach until it curved, then they were to angle toward the buildings. Del, Leonada and Click were going to head along the path they'd taken before while Solaria and Yul, the other Tursiops mover, would slip south and then cut in toward the buildings. Solaria had explained that by breaking up their group, they had a better chance of at least one of them making it through to the buildings and getting the intel they needed without getting caught.

"You know," Gal said as he and Skylar started off down the beach with Filzbalm flying along beside them, "I can't say I've ever seen or heard of a Solar Drake before."

"I'd be surprised if you had.Del found information about him, but it was really hard to do." Skylar didn't want to explain how much time Del had spent on the shadow web before Filzbalm was hatched, or after as they tried to find out where he was from. "He's not unique, but there aren't a lot of Solar Drakes, and most of them never leave their home planet."

"Sounds like there's a story there," Gal said. "Maybe I'll stop by sometime and you or Del can fill me in. If you don't mind."

"That might be fun." Skylar glanced back as Filzbalm came swooping in.

"We look fairly clear," Filzbalm announced as he circled Skylar's head once, then flew back toward the buildings. *"I didn't go too far, just in case."*

"That's fine. Keep scouting and let me know if you spot anything." Skylar turned off the beach and headed the way Filzbalm was flying.

"And he's telepathic, I guess," Gal said, following Skylar.

"Very." Skylar ducked under a low-hanging branch. "Keeps life interesting."

"Then he's also pretty smart, huh?" Gal continued to chatter.

"That too." Skylar wondered why Click had picked Gal for the mission if he didn't know how to shut up. Any Boarisk out patrolling the island were sure to hear him. "We're getting close."

"Oh." Gal sounded like he got the hint.

In the night-dark forest, Filzbalm didn't leave any signs of his passage. Every so often, something would pass between Skylar and a spot of light from the buildings. It was fleeting and he assumed it was the little Solar Drake. There was enough moonlight that even after they left the beach, finding their way wasn't hard, although Skylar wished that either Solaria or Leonada was with him as their night vision was extremely keen. They'd decided to not use night vision equipment for fear the Boarisk might have EM-detecting tech that would pick up the faint signals from the goggles. Del had assured him that Tursiops had fairly decent night vision, not Pantherian quality, but better than humans.

"Hold up," Gal hissed in Skylar's ear.

"What?" Skylar kept his eyes opened.

"There's someone out here," Gal said at the same that Filzbalm spoke in Skyler's mind.

Skylar scanned the jungle but didn't spot anything that looked like a problem. "Where?" he asked in the barest whisper.

Gal pointed off to their right. "Over there."

"Then let's swing the other way." Skylar took off to the left, moving much slower than before, and keeping his eyes and ears open for anything that would tell him where the trouble might come from.

"It's a Boarisk guard," Filzbalm said. *"I don't think he spotted you. He's still walking the direction he had been."*

"Good." Skylar sighed softly in relief. "The guard is still walking, but away from us," he whispered, so Gal would know what Filzbalm told him.

"That's good. Your Solar Drake is really handy."

"Most of the time." Skylar grinned to himself as he thought about some of the trouble Filzbalm could get into when he was being overly curious about something new. He didn't feel handy then, just like a big menace in a small orange and yellow body.

"I hardly get into the amount of trouble you're capable of." Filzbalm sounded a little indignant and it brought a smile to Skylar, helping to momentarily lighten the mood.

They made it to the edge of the compound without further incident. Skylar knew better than to relax, though. The deeper they got into enemy territory, the more potential danger they were in. They didn't have the storm to cover them. All they had were their wits and their psychic skills, and against Boarisk, only the movers had any chance of making an impact.

Skylar squatted at the edge of the jungle and studied the compound. In the moonlight it looked different than it had in the storm. The buildings appeared closer together, and there were more of them. From what he could tell there were at least a dozen, if not more.

He closed his eyes to block out anything that might distract him, then reached his mind out to Solaria and Del. They'd been in mental rapport often enough that he found their thoughts easily.

"We've reached the edge of the jungle on the south side of the compound," Skylar reported.

"We've been sitting here on the north side for a while now," Solaria replied. *"Haven't seen much, just a couple of guards who were easy enough to evade."*

"Same here," Del joined in. *"But there do seem to be more of them around than before."*

"They're out because there's no storm going on," Solaria reminded him.

"Del, you're probably closest to the buildings we went into last time. Do you want to try sneaking over, getting a crate, and heading back? Then Solaria and Click and Gal and I can head into the compound and see what we can find in our respective areas."

"Okay. The crate is priority. Keep an eye out."

"Filzbalm, can you fly over and help Del?" Skylar suggested.

"Sure." There was a soft flutter of leathery wings from closer than Skylar expected. He almost jumped, but reminded himself that he needed to be quiet.

"Sneaky little guy, isn't he?" Gal muttered near Skylar's ear.

"Yeah," Skylar whispered back.

"You're all clear," Filzbalm said in the link between the others. With everyone joined, his voice wasn't nearly as loud as it normally was when he was trying to get more than just Skylar to hear him.

Skylar looked in the direction he was pretty sure Del was in. There was a bit of movement in the moonlight. Three figures dashed from the tree line toward the closest building. Then he saw a flash of movement as something small flew high across the same stretch.

"They've got new locks and sensors," Del said. *"We must've spooked them when we were here during the storm. Click and Leonada are handling them. I'd ask Astara, but there's a chance they'd pick up on her."*

"If it's too complicated, we'll wait on crates and see what else we can find out about the compound." Skylar didn't want the alarms going off and alerting the island's inhabitants to their presence.

"No worries, Leonada took out the electronic alarms and Click got the big lock open. The lock looks antique. I'm bringing it along to figure out how it works. Might be mechanical as opposed to electronic." Del sounded excited about the lock, which made Skylar hope he didn't get too distracted and miss something important. Del was all about new things, sometimes to the exclusion of everything else around him.

"Just stay focused," Skylar said, trying to spread his senses out to spot any non-Boarisk minds. There were small clusters of minds not far from him. A couple of the minds seemed stronger than the others, like they had some level of psi abilities. He hadn't been trained to tell exactly how strong other psis were just by brushing against their minds.

"We've got a crate," Del said. *"Yul says it's just within his limits, Leonada is helping him out. We're heading back to Astara."*

"Sounds good," Solaria said. *"Skylar, do we want to wait for them to get back to Astara before we go farther into the compound, or go ahead?"*

Skylar wasn't sure how to answer. He'd suddenly ended up in charge. They were looking for him to lead. He'd never meant to lead anyone, but since Pantheria, he'd grown in his power—they all had, but he was the one who could pull everyone together. Somehow, he found himself with them defaulting to him because most psychics defaulted to the strongest to lead them. He hadn't planned on it, but that was how things panned out.

"Let's go at the same time. Stay in contact." Skylar felt like it made sense to move quickly.

"They've got the crate and heading back," Skylar said as he glanced at Gal. "Let's check out this first building."

"I'm right behind you," Gal said.

A flutter of wings heralded Filzbalm's return. *"You're clear between here and the building,"* the Solar Drake's voice rang through their link.

"Thanks." Skylar dashed from the cover of the jungle to the closest building. He felt exposed as he ran, but he trusted Filzbalm to know what was going on. Filzbalm would keep them covered.

13
Down The Boarisk Hole

WITH FILZBALM'S directions, Skylar and Gal made it around to the building's door without being seen. The coarse outside of the building was some form of recycled plascrete. More than a few buildings back on Hummassa were made of the stuff—it was resistant to rot in a humid climate, and made good use of waste materials.

The moon was bright enough for him to almost make out details in the shadows it cast. As they left the jungle covering and hurried across the few yards to the building, Skylar realized what had been missing from the tropical experience: there were no sounds of insects. He had always heard a myriad of insects, birds and other night creatures back on Hummassa, but they were missing on Tursipia. On a water world, maybe anything that wasn't tied to the ocean simply didn't evolve there.

Approaching the door, he pushed the idea out of his head. He needed to focus on their mission and could worry about the lack of bugs later.

"We're still clear," Filzbalm announced, his voice in Skylar's head causing him to jump slightly. He'd been so lost in his pondering of bugs he'd lost track. That wasn't good.

"Thanks." Skylar tried the door.

It was unlocked.

Hoping it wouldn't squeak as he opened it, Skylar eased the door wide enough for him and Gal to slip in.

"Filzbalm, stay on the roof and keep a lookout," Skylar said as he paused, hoping his eyes would adjust to

the darkness in the building and he wouldn't have to worry about using his palm light.

"*Will do.*"

"Not much in here," Gal said softly.

"What do you see?" Skylar still couldn't make out anything, but knew Tursiops had better night vision than most baseline humans. They could handle dark ocean depths, plus had echo location they could rely on. But since he wasn't hearing any clicks from Gal, Skylar didn't think he was using that ability.

"A lot of boxes. Like this place is used for storage."

Skylar had been hoping for something more, like an office, barracks, or an electronics room like they'd found last time. But as he thought about it, storage made sense if the Boarisk were harvesting or plundering something from the ocean floor. They had to put it somewhere until they were ready to take it off world. If they were moving a lot of it, a good number of the buildings would be storage.

"Let's try another building," Skylar said softly.

"*We've got nothing in our first one,*" Solarai said through their group link. "*We're heading to the next building over.*"

"*Same here. We'll wait until you're in your building before we move,*" Skylar responded. "Wait a minute, Solaria and Click are moving now." He leaned against one of the crates that he could just barely make out in the darkness.

"*We're still clear,*" Filzbalm said. "*But there are people moving in the jungle, coming this way.*"

Skylar's heartbeat picked up. "*Can you tell anything about them?*" He knew it would have been too easy to get in, get info, and get out without anybody noticing them, but he'd hoped to get at least a little farther and have some knowledge to pass along before they had to run.

"Not yet. I'll fly that way and see what I can find out."

The Solar Drake taking off without Skylar along made a chill pass through him. He didn't want anything to happen to Filzbalm. He glanced at Gal. "Filzbalm's going to keep watch for us outside while we head into the buildings." He kept his voice low.

Gal nodded.

"We've made it to the next building," Solaria announced.

"We're back at Astara," Del told everyone. *"Should we return to the compound?"*

"No," Skylar said. *"Stay on the ship. If we're not all back in an hour, take the crate to Professor Aduncus and let him figure out the next move."*

"Okay. We'll get the crate secured so we can take off as soon as everyone's on board." Del didn't sound happy about being told to stay back with the ship, but Skylar didn't want too many people wandering around in the jungle, multiplying their chances of getting caught.

"We're heading to the next building." Skylar opened the door slightly, wishing Filzbalm was still on the roof above them.

With Gal shadowing him, Skylar scurried along the outside of the storage building and then paused at the corner. He checked all around before dashing for the next building. He didn't like the way the moon cast a long shadow on the sand as he ran. If anyone was paying attention to perimeter cameras, they'd be sure to notice something. *"Del, can we get Astara to block their security network, or something? I'm feeling exposed."*

"Getting on it. She tried something earlier, but I think they've upped their safegaurds since we were here last and she wasn't able to get very far into them."

"Do what you two can."

Gal made it across the space and there still wasn't anyone shooting at them.

"There are three Boarisk on patrol with heavy rifles," Filzbalm said. *"They are just clearing the trees now. They're following your footprints in the sand."*

With his hand on the door, Skylar paused and looked down. They hadn't even thought about leaving footprints in the island's soft sand. *"Crap."* "Gal, can you use your mover powers to scatter the sand behind us, erase out footprints? Filzbalm says there's a Boarisk patrol following them."

Gal nodded. "Sure thing."

A tingle of power came out of him. It felt a little like Solaria using her mover gifts but was subtler. The sand behind them moved in a soft wave. Where they'd walked suddenly looked just like the rest of the compound's ground.

The door was unlocked and Skylar pushed it open and as soon as they made it in the building, Gal moved the sand, erasing evidence of their passage.

As he closed the door, a feeling of being trapped hit Skylar. They'd made it to the building, but if there was a Boarisk patrol looking for them, it was only a matter of time before one of them checked all the buildings for intruders. If they thought to call for more help, the whole compound would be crawling with Boarisk before too long. Their quiet night invasion was about to go horribly wrong.

"We made it to the building," Skylar told everyone in the link. *"But we might have a problem."*

"Astara was able to jam their coms," Del said. *"They aren't going to be able to use them to call for help, but help isn't far away. If they start shooting, more guards will show up. We're working on coming up with something to cause a bit more confusion to give us cover. It might be time to beat feet."*

"That's probably a good idea," Solaria said. *"We can get the crate back to the professor and then see about coming back and finding out more info. Maybe approach a different strategy in this hunt."*

"We've got more crates," Gal said. "But there's a hatch in the floor over here."

Skylar wanted to investigate that hatch and see where it led. *"Solaria, you and Click get back to Astara. We just found a hatch in a storage building. Gal and I are going to investigate it and will then see about getting out so we can leave."*

"The patrol didn't find you in the other building and has just realized their coms are down." Filzbalm announced. *"They're fanning out to check other buildings."*

"Then we better get into this hatch and see where it leads." Skylar looked at the cut-out in the floor. It didn't look like a door so much as lines cut out of the smooth plascrete that made up the floor, but it was different from the large interlocking tiles of the rest of the surface beneath their feet. "Can you pull that up, or are you going to need help?"

Gal shrugged. "Won't know until I try. Depends on what they have weighing it down, or if there's a latch of some kind." He extended his hand toward the door, in a gesture Skylar recognized from Solaria and other movers he'd been around, as a way for him to focus his power. The tingle of psi energy ran across Skylar's body and the square hatch slowly rose from the other tiles. Gal's brow creased in concentration.

"Okay, there's a latch, trying to get it open." Gal said.

Skylar pushed his reader senses out, trying to tell if there were any active minds below them. He paused, shocked, as he brushed against a number of minds. They weren't directly below the hatch, but deeper, in the lower part of the island. From what Del had told him about the Tursiopian constructed islands, they were similar to ships, with a large part of them under the water. They already knew from Astara's scans there were tubes leading from the lower parts of the island to habitats on the sea floor. He hadn't expected to encounter so many minds down there.

"We're clear directly below us," Skylar said softly. "But there are people out from there."

"Then down you go." Gal's power wrapped around Skylar and lowered him into the dark hole.

It wasn't the first time a mover had lifted him, but Skylar still found the sensation of floating down, or up, to be very disorienting. He wanted to hold on to something, but there wasn't anything there. He glanced around in the darkened hole and couldn't see a ladder, a lift, or anything that should've been there to move people or goods up into the storage building. Moments after the hatch closed above them, Skylar's feet touched the floor.

"Okay," Gal said softly as he followed Skylar. "I think it's time for some light. I can't see anything."

"They just entered the building you're in," Filzbalm reported. *"They are getting more and more agitated."*

Skylar turned on his palm light and looked that direction. A short tunnel led away from the shaft they'd just come down. "Let's go this way." He started away from the shaft.

As they entered the tunnel, there was a click from the hatch, and a beam of light shined down. Skylar turned off his palm light, pressed himself against the wall, and stayed as still as he could. Gal did the same. They were far enough into the tunnel that the light never reached them. After a couple of seconds, the light went away and the hatch closed.

Skylar waited several seconds after the hatch closed before he let out the breath he'd been holding. "That was close."

"Might get a lot closer," Gal muttered. "Really wondering what Click talked us into."

Skylar didn't bother reminding him it wasn't Click who had planned out the mission. Sure, Click had talked Gal and Yul into coming along, but they were there because Skylar and his friends had discovered the island and wanted to stop the Boarisk.

"We can handle it." Skylar squared his shoulders and turned the palm light back on. He wished they had two of them, but one seemed to be enough for Gal.

The tunnel ended in a door. It was locked.

Turned and looked at Gal. "Can you open this? Solaria's gotten good at unlocking things."

Gal nodded. "Even first level movers can unlock most mechanical locks. That's one of the big reasons why so many modern locks are electronic." He stepped in front of Skylar, knelt down and stared at the lock. The bit of power he pushed out was barely tangible. Then there was a soft click. He stood and pushed the door open. "There we go."

"That patrol is leaving your building," Filzbalm announced. *"They're even more agitated now than they were before. They're heading toward the building where the com systems were during the storm. You might not have much more time."*

They were making headway on exploring the place. Skylar didn't want to give up so soon. He wanted to keep digging and see about finding everything he could before they returned to Astara.

"We've made it back to the jungle," Solaria said. *"Should be back to Astara in five to seven minutes."*

"The patrols seem to be heading back to the main compound," Del said. *"Their tech person is trying to*

bypass Astara's shutdown on their coms. We need to get moving."

"*Give us a little more time,*" Skylar said, trying not to sound like he was pleading. "*If they start heading your way, take off. Maybe if they see you leaving they'll relax and give us some space.*" But he didn't like the idea of being stuck on the island with angry Boarisk hunting for him.

"*No way,*" Solaria said. "*If you're in trouble, we're coming for you.*"

"*She's right,*" Del echoed.

"*No, actually this is a good idea. Get the crate to the professor. Maybe if the council sees hard proof of something going on, they'll finally take action to shut it down. Gal and I will be fine.*" Skylar did his best to sound strong and confident. "*Filzbalm is still outside. He can keep an eye on things there.*"

As Skylar stepped into the door and panned his light across the area in there, his breath caught. There were eyes staring back at him from the light. Eyes of every shape and color. The faces they were set in were unreadable, but a surge of hope radiated off the people they'd found.

14
Saving The Past

SKYLAR STOOD there for a moment as he and Gal stared at the group of people staring back at them.

An older man, from a species Skylar wasn't familiar with, walked up to them. "You shouldn't be here." His almond-shaped purple eyes were hazy and his orange skin seemed to hang from his face, giving him exaggerated jowls. Black cuffs were around the man's wrists, but he didn't appear bound in any way.

"Are you slaves of the Boarisk?" Skylar asked.

"It appears that way on the surface," the man said.

A woman with dark red skin pushed her way to the front of the group. "Let me through." Her voice was very familiar.

Skylar's heart skipped a beat. "Taglia? Taglia Puddle?"

"Skylar!" The woman cleared the edge of the group and rushed up to him. "Skylar Mars, how did you get here?"

Skylar picked the woman up in a hug. "Taglia. Oh, gods, Taglia. I can't believe it." He tried to catch his breath, but had difficulties as emotions warred within him. Taglia Puddle was Teir's mother. She'd been lost in the Boarisk attack on Hummassa when Skylar's mother was killed.

When he stopped hugging her, she stepped back and looked at him. "Skylar, you've gotten so big." She grabbed his hands and stared at them. "You're not a slave here. How is that possible?"

"Is that what these mean?" Skylar touched her black bracelets. "You're a slave?"

She nodded. "We all are."

"Skylar, what's going on?" Del called. *"Your emotions are all over the place."*

"I just found Teir's mother. She's a slave here." Skylar knew he wasn't going to leave the island without her, and any other sentients who were also enslaved.

"Then we have to get them out," Solaria said.

Skylar looked at the many other people standing around them. There were too many to get them all off on Astara. *"We're going to need a bigger ship. Go back to the Professor. Tell him we've found slaves here. Show him the crate. At least come back with the Diver, but try for more. Gal, Filzbalm, and I will work on getting everyone free."*

"There're a lot more guards coming out of that building they all went into," Filzbalm said. *"I don't think you should try to get out now."*

"I'm staying on the island with you and Filzbalm," Solaria said. *"I might be of some help from topside. Del and the others can head back, then return with help."*

"Grandfather and Ms. Grissom aren't going to like this," Del said.

"Too bad. It's happening. I'll grab some supplies and stay here."

Solaria's insistence on staying made a warm spot spread through Skylar. She was willing to help him save the people who'd been so important to him in the past.

"Filzbalm, head over and help Solaria until we need your eyes in the sky again," Skylar said. *"We're going to make this happen."*

"On my way," Filzbalm said.

"Skylar, are you okay?" Taglia asked, waving her hand in front of his eyes.

"Give him a second," Gal said. "He's probably talking with the others."

Skylar nodded as he blinked. "Yeah. Sorry about that, Taglia. A lot's changed since Hummassa. I had to let my friends on the surface know we found you. They're going to head out and get more help." He glanced at Gal. "Solaria and Filzbalm are staying in case we need help from the surface."

Taglia frowned. "You weren't using a com—coms down here require a special frequency, or at least that's what the guards tell the new people."

"No." Skylar shook his head. "After the attack, I discovered some things about myself. Look, that's not really important right now. We need to know what's going on and then make a plan on how to get you all out."

"There is no out," the old man said. "Even if we don't turn you over to the Boarisk, you'll be slaves soon enough. Nobody ever leaves these islands."

Taglia punched him in the shoulder. "Enough out of you, Zelion. I won't have you scaring Skylar. If he says there's a chance for a rescue, then we're going to believe him."

Her confidence in him was tangible to Skylar's feeler abilities. It was almost the same pride he often felt coming off Solaria's mother Felonia. In many ways, Taglia had been like a second mother to him on Hummassa, and he suddenly missed his own mother more than he had in months.

"Taglia, where's Teir? Is he here with you? Intergal Rescue never found evidence of any of you." Skylar desperately hoped Teir was there. It would be so great to be able to rescue his friend as well.

Sadness suddenly replaced her confidence. "He *was* here, but I haven't seen him in several months. He was taken away with the other youngsters who were showing promise, or at least that's what the Orcan who took them said."

A stab of fear went through Skylar. "So the Orcans are involved in this. We knew the islands were in the oceans they claimed." Skylar ran a hand through his hair. "Did they say what kind of promise they showed?"

Taglia shook her head. "They treat us as little more than animals. They don't tell us more than they need to."

"And in many ways we are little more than animals," Zelion mumbled.

Taglia glared at him. "Speak for yourself. Some of us still remember what we were before the Boarisk got their grubby hands on us. Not all of us have been beaten into submission to the level you have. I held on to hope." She looked at Skylar. "I just never dreamed it would come in the form of a young man who's almost my son."

"Look, this is great and all, but we need to start figuring out what's going on here, and how to get out," Gal grumbled from behind Skylar.

"Right. We're also going to need to find Teir and the others that were taken away. If they're still on this island, we've got to get to them and free them too." Skylar's hatred for the Boarisk grew. They were a diabolical species that didn't deserve to share the universe with the rest of the kinder, gentler peoples. He looked at Taglia. "What are they getting from the bottom of the ocean?"

"All the metals we can pull out," she said. "There are mines going deep into the crust. I doubt even Zelion has even been to all of them."

"And who would want to?" the old slave spat. "Every one of them is just the same. Death traps."

Skylar was taking it all in, and it was a lot. He tried to figure out what they should do first. He didn't want any of the slaves to be hurt because he and Gal were there. If any of them said anything, they'd probably all suffer. He had to free Taglia, and wanted to find Teir, but other lives hung in the balance too. The Boarisk had taken so much from him and he had a chance to get some of it back, but was it worth the risk to others? If he tried to free Taglia and the others before they searched for Teir, there was too much of a chance of everything being discovered and things getting messy.

He wasn't used to being put in this kind of situation. Even when he'd been playing Galactic Explorers with Teir or Del, they had never been faced with such a complex problem that could end up hurting so many people if they made the wrong decision.

"Solaria, I need to figure out what to do." He reached out to his friend through the link that felt strangely empty with Del gone from it. Although he might've been able to hold the link at a great distance, he figured Del had dropped out when he'd gotten Astara airborne and headed back to Aduncus Island.

"What's up?" She sounded oddly cheerful. The mood didn't fit with the way Skylar felt. *"Filzbalm and I are on the way back to the compound. Got supplies, even a few extra stimpatches—you know, for emergencies."*

Inwardly, Skylar groaned. He knew how powerful Solaria was without the added stimulation of the chemical patches to boost her mover skills. She'd been pushing the patches since using the first one back on Pantheria. No matter how much she kept telling everyone she wasn't becoming an addict, Skylar wasn't sure.

Pushing his concern for her aside before she caught it through their mental connection, Skylar laid out what they had learned.

Solaria was silent for a moment.

"Okay. Right now, I think we need to leave the slaves where they are. Ask them not to tell the Boarisk or the Orcans about your visit to their little piece of Hell. You and Gal keep going deeper into the mines, island, I don't know exactly what to call it." She paused. *"Let*

them know they are going to need to be ready when you come back through. They may have to move fast."

"If we've got support from Professor Aduncus, they are going to have *to move fast before the Boarisk figure out we're here and make escape that much harder. Hey, I just thought of something—since we're dealing with Orcans as well as Boarisk, then they'll be susceptible to telepathy. We can influence them."* Finding at least one weakness made Skylar feel a bit better about their situation.

"But if the prey has the same ability as the hunter it levels the hunting ground," Solaria said. *"We're going to have to be more careful, even with our mind-to-mind communications. The Orcans might have a powerful reader on their payroll who'll be able to pick up on us."*

Skylar hadn't thought of that. It ended his momentary cheer quickly. They were going to have to be careful. *"Right. Okay. You and Filzbalm stay in the jungle and keep a thought out for me. We're going to keep pushing our way deeper into this mess and see what we can find."*

"We will." Their joined voice rang oddly through his head, then they were gone.

He looked at Taglia and Zelion, then past them to the others pressing close. "Okay. Gal and I are going to head in deeper and see what more we can find, who we can find. If Teir and the others who were taken with him are still on this island, or in the habitats on the ocean floor, we're going to find them, free them, and bring them home."

Taglia hugged Skylar. "You be careful, Skylar. Knowing you're alive and well has been the best news I've had in months. Stay that way."

"All of you too," Skylar said. "Don't let on that we're here, and we'll come back this way once my friends arrive with enough transport to get all of you free."

He hoped he wasn't going to let all of these people down. He would have to do everything he could to make sure Taglia and the rest of them were saved. Skylar crossed his fingers and hoped Professor Aduncus would be able to get someone from the government to believe him and bring lots of help quickly.

15
Of War And Showers

SKYLAR NEARLY bumped into Taglia as she stopped at a doorway. He was thankful Gal was paying more attention and didn't hit him.

"What's wrong?" Skylar whispered. Since leaving the room where the slaves were kept in the dark, Taglia had been leading them deeper into the island.

"This is as far as I can go." She held up her wrist. "If I go any farther, these will activate and blow my arms off."

"What?" Skylar stared at her, trying to comprehend how someone would be so cruel to anyone, even people they viewed as slaves. If their slaves didn't have any arms, they couldn't do any work—not to mention the explosion would probably kill them. "Why would they do that?"

"Terror." Taglia gave Skylar a quick hug. "They keep us docile by terror. Now, go. Find Teir and the others. Until you reach the lift shaft, there is no direct way down. Be careful and don't get caught." She stepped back and looked at him in the light of his palmlight. "I don't want to lose you again."

Skylar gave her a slight smile—it was all he could work up in the wake of the fear and concern coming off her. "I'll be fine. If Gal lets anything happen to me, I have a friend who's going to tear him apart."

"He's right," Gal said softly.

Taglia fixed him with a look. "As will I." Then she turned and hurried off toward the room they'd found her in. With his feeler gift, Skylar could tell she was crying.

He shook his head, trying to clear the emotions running through him. After see Hummassans on the beach during the storm, Skylar had hoped to find some of the natives from his birth-world on the island, but he'd never expected to find Teir or his family there. It was just too much of coincidence. He reminded himself he was in a dangerous situation and needed to keep his head on straight.

The door was locked.

"Gal?" Skylar stepped to the side to let the Tursipian mover at the door.

"I'm still amazed they aren't using elocks. These Boarisk are backwater. But if they're running with Orcans, what else can we expect?" He fell silent, and a moment later, there was a small click. Then he opened the door.

"You're not a fan of Orcans?" Skylar pushed the door opened and slipped into another dark corridor. There were rows of faint lights running along the floor. They were enough to see the floor, but not enough to illuminate the place.

Skylar panned his palmlight around the space. It was a hallway that went farther than the light reached.

"Most Tursiops aren't," Gal said. "They've tried to assume control of the planet several times. They're bigger and more dangerous than the rest of us, but we have a lot more people than they do. That's always tipped the odds in our favor."

"Del never said anything about the Orcans trying to take over the planet," Skylar said as they started down the corridor.

Gal shook his head. "Probably wouldn't. I love Click and his family, but they tend to see the good in everyone. Honestly, I was surprised when Click asked Yul and me to come on this mission. It's very unlike them to take the first steps in what could become a war if things go badly. With the Orcans involved, there's a good chance it will."

The last thing Skylar wanted to do was start a war. Sure, he wanted to make the Boarisk pay for what they'd done to Hummassa, and after finding Taglia and the other slaves, he wanted that more than anything, but he couldn't imagine plunging an entire world into conflict. It didn't make sense. He hoped they'd be able to pull off the rescue without that.

The hallway ended in another door.

"Let me try it first," Gal said, stepping up to it and pushing against it. It didn't budge. "Okay. I'll get this done." He squatted down and stared at the spot where the door met the wall. A slow grin spread across his face.

"What's up?" Skylar asked, fairly sure this was the longest it had taken Gal to open a lock to that point.

"Elock. Finally. Modern tech." He let out a slow breath. "Now, let's see if I can open this without setting off the alarms."

"Is there anything I can do?" Skylar asked, although he was pretty sure there wasn't.

"Just stand there and watch our backs." Gal put his hand on the lock. "Actually, can you scan the other side of this and make sure we're not heading into a squad of pig dudes or something else that's going to blow our heads off the second it opens?"

"Sure." Skylar nodded, then closed his eyes and pushed his thoughts out beyond the door. It felt fairly empty, but then Boarisk didn't normally show up on psychic scans. Being immune to readers and feelers also tended to make them fairly invisible. "I think we're clear."

"Good. I think I got it." There was no click, but Gal straightened and pushed the door open. "Actually, Elocks are easier than mechanical, if you're good at moving electrons around. The hard part is making sure you don't open the circuit the wrong way and trigger an alarm. I almost did that."

"But you got us in." Skylar said, and eased past Gal to get a look at the room beyond the door.

There were actually lights on in this one. The place looked like a lockerroom, complete with showers and lockers. There were white lab suits there—similar to envirosuits, but without the ability to withstand the rigors of space.

"Not much privacy in this place," Gal noted. "I bet this is for the slaves."

"But why the showers and lab suits?" Skylar walked over to one of the suits hanging on a plastic hanger at the end of a long rack of them.

"Didn't they say the pigs are mining down here?" Gal walked over to the lockers.

"Yeah, but these don't look like anything I've seen in text books about mining. This looks like a processing lab of some sort." Skylar touched the suit—it was more cloth than metal fiber, strictly for indoor use.

"If they are mining precious metals from the planet's crust, then maybe they're trying to make sure none of the minerals get out of the lab, or processing area." Gal stepped away from the lockers. "If they have the slaves totally clean themselves between shifts, they won't lose anything precious. Look at these." He pointed at several large upright tubes at the end of the showers. "I bet these are driers of some kind. There aren't any towels around that we can see. If the slaves go from the showers to the driers, even if a little bit of dust got caught in their hair or scales, the pigs would retrieve it."

Skylar stared at the clear tubes. There were grates on the tops and bottoms of them, perfect for forcing air through at high velocities. "That makes sense. But the thing that's been bugging me since we talked to the slaves"—he resisted saying Taglia's name, it made things too personal and he knew if he stepped back and kept things clinical, he'd be able to think better—"I thought planetary mining had been outlawed centuries ago. Most systems have enough minerals in asteroids that are easier to get to."

"It must be something special," Gal said. "They didn't say what they were mining."

Skylar nodded. "That's right." An idea hit him. He turned and looked at the suits. "These things have hoods. I wonder if we can use them to slip into the area and find out more about what's going on."

"Might work, or it might not." Gal frowned toward the suits. "If the suits are bio-coded, they'll only work for one person. Or if the pigs have any kind of sensor in the suits they might not work for us."

"But wouldn't it be better than wandering around here as ourselves?" Skylar asked. "I mean, we'd be safer, right?"

"No." Gal shook his head. "I don't like it. Not if they have a work pattern or something like that. They did say something about the other shift, didn't they? That means they come and go, but as a group."

It all felt really daunting. "Okay. So what if we wait for the shift change? We don't know how long it's going to be before Del brings back help. If we wait for a shift change we can use two of the suits to disguise ourselves and just blend in with the others."

Before Gal could answer, the door they came through slowly opened. Skylar's heart pounded as he glanced at Gal.

"Behind the lockers," Gal hissed, and pointed as he took off running as quietly as possible on the solid plastcrete floor.

Skylar followed, trying to get a feeling for who was coming in. There were at least two people—one of them must've been Boarisk since Skylar couldn't pick up anything about him except through his brush with the other one. The one Skylar could read was an Orcan. He was irritated by something.

Gal grabbed Skylar's arm and pulled him toward a narrow door behind the lockers. "In here." His voice was barely audible.

Skylar slid into the space, a small closet, as Gal pulled the door almost shut. Skylar hoped they would hear something over the beating of his heart.

16
First Blood

SKYLAR CLICKED off his palmlight after realizing it was still spilling light into the darkness. He didn't want anything to give them away as they huddled there while two people walked across the locker room a few feet away. The door was open just enough they could still hear them. The closet was stuffy, and Skylar really wished there was a little more space for him and Gal.

"There's no way we've got people on the island," the Orcan said, his voice smooth and easy, reminiscent of most Tursiops.

"They were here during the storm." The Boarisk's voice was coarse, like trying to talk around his tusk gave him a heavy lisp. "I was on the beach. I saw them lifting off, but they vanished quickly."

"Our instruments aren't detecting anyone that shouldn't be here," the Orcan countered.

The Boarisk huffed. "Instruments aren't infallible. Can *you* pick up anything?"

A mind brushed against Skylar's. He shut himself down the way he'd been taught and hoped it was enough that he wouldn't be detected. He wasn't sure how much training Gal had beyond Mover classes.

"Nothing," the Orcan muttered. "I thought there was something there for a moment, but it might've been one of the prospects trying to master their new abilities. I don't know." For several seconds the only sound was their shoes on the tile floor, then the Orcan continued. "The sooner we get finished going through this part of the island, the sooner we can get outside. I hate these underground areas. I can tell we're underwater, even though we're dry. It feels weird."

"You Orcans are too sensitive," the Boarisk said. "There's nothing wrong with being underground. It's a lot like being in space."

"I don't like that either," the Orcan said. "We need to get finished up here so I can go back to spending my time on the beach."

"We're done when the bosses say we're done," the Boarisk replied. A door squeaked open, then closed, cutting off the conversation.

Skylar breathed a sigh of relief. If the Orcan had been a better reader, or more intent on his job, the odds were very good he would've picked up on Skylar and Gal being there. He obviously didn't like the underside of the island and was fairly sloppy. Knowing more than a few Tursiops, Skylar was a little surprised by that. If both races were evolved from similar creatures from Sol Three, it seemed as though they should've been more alike.

"Well that didn't tell us much," Gal muttered close by Skylar's shoulder.

"Nope." Skylar wanted to get out of the closet, but they needed to give the others a little more time to get down the hall or wherever they were going. "Other than give us undeniable proof the Orcans are working with the Boarisks."

Gal sighed. "And that's bad on several levels. Orcans have never been known for their ability to be upstanding citizens. They've been trying to find a way to break the treaty with the Resmordians for generations. They claim they should be in charge."

"Was that what their wars were fought over?" Skylar asked.

"It might've been at the core of the conflict," Gal replied. "But their fight with *us* was always over territory. The funny thing is, after each war, they actually lost ground—or maybe I should say islands, or water."

Skylar scratched his head and opened the door just a little farther. He didn't hear anyone about. He reached out with his mind and didn't feel anyone close by. "We're clear. I wonder if this island is one they had *lost* but didn't want to surrender. Del thought it might be one that had been reported destroyed in a storm, but if the Orcans have been finding a way to hide it."

As they eased out of the closet, Gal pursed his lips and looked thoughtful. "I guess that's possible, but they would've had to deactivate the island's transponder. Each island has a beacon that lets the planet's security satellites know where they are."

"That shouldn't have been too hard," Skylar said. "Plenty of different ways to deactivate, or even disguise a signal." Since they'd gotten Astara free of the AI Armada's network and given her a new life, they'd all gotten to understand how transponders and other communications on ships worked. For such a major security feature, they were ridiculously easy to interrupt or change if the need arose.

Gal glanced around the room. "Right. Okay, so do we follow them, or see about finding a different door to go through?"

"Not sure." Skylar really wished they had a map of the lower part of the island. As it was they were just going to have to wander around until they found Teir or the others who'd been taken and hope they didn't run across the patrol that had come through the locker room. "We need to keep moving. What do you think?"

"Why don't we follow those guys until we find another passageway we can go down?" Gal started for the door the two guards had gone through. "The Orcan was right, it does feel strange down here—under the water, but still dry."

"Okay. I didn't hear them lock or unlock the door, so hopefully we can get through quickly."

Gal pushed against the door. "Yeah, it's open." He opened it slowly, then paused. "Another hallway. I don't see or hear anyone."

"Good. What about doors?" Skylar wanted to be in front of Gal but didn't want to get too pushy about it.

"Nope. Goes down a bit and looks like it T's." Gal took a couple of steps into the hall, then eased over giving Skylar a better look at the hallway. It was lit, where the others hadn't been. It seemed to go down about ten to twelve feet, then came to a T.

Without a word, they crept down the hallway. Skylar moved in a careful heel-toe fashion Solaria had taught him, claiming it was quieter than walking tip-toe. The drawback was that it was slower.

At the end of the hall they paused. Skylar did a light mental scan down both directions. He didn't want to let the Orcan know they were there, but wanted to go the way the two guards hadn't. There was nothing for him to read. Not from guards, anyway. It sounded like there was another group of slaves heading their way from the tunnel on the left. Since they were in a hallway coming from the locker room, they might be heading toward the showers, but Skylar wasn't sure. They could've just been continuing down the hallway and would be following Skylar and Gal. He'd feel better with the slaves behind them, if that turned out to be the case.

"Let's go right." Skylar wasn't sure how a second group of slaves would react to them, particularly if he didn't know any of them.

"Okay." Gal turned and walked next to Skylar as they headed away from the locker room and the group of slaves. If they were lucky, they would find the slaves again in the room where Taglia and the others had been.

SEVERAL HALLWAYS down, they finally started finding rooms with various equipment in them, but neither Skylar or Gal had any idea what the stuff was good for. Skylar wished Del was there since he might've had some clue as to what they were dealing with.

Gal shut the lid on a crate with something that might've been a motor of some kind—at least, it looked like it had pistons and a combustion chamber, but that didn't make a lot of sense to Skylar since internal combustion engines had been outlawed centuries earlier as sources of pollution and extremely inefficient as new and better technologies came along.

"I've got no clue," Gal said. "This equipment is new, or at least looks new, but the tech is outdated."

"Maybe they're trying to cut corners on things," Skylar suggested as he closed another box of similar stuff. "Maybe…" He shook his head. "I've got no idea. This is just getting weirder and weirder."

Nearby, a door opened.

Skylar's heart nearly stopped. He frantically gestured for Gal to get behind the stack of boxes they'd been looking through. He'd felt strange opening the first one. It wasn't his stuff, after all—then he reminded himself that he wasn't supposed to be on the island. But it was an island that didn't officially exist in the first place, and the Boarisk were on Tursipia without permission for the planetary government. If anything they discovered helped them get the Boarisk off the planet, he decided it was all fair game.

Another team of two guards came through the door at the far end of the room. Their footfalls seemed to come straight toward the pile of boxes Skylar and Gal were behind.

"Nothing looks out of place," said one, a Boarisk, based on his gruff voice. "The silent alarms must be malfunctioning."

Skylar closed his eyes and inwardly groaned. Either he or Gal should've thought about silent alarms. He wondered how many they'd triggered as they'd gone from room to room looking for anything they could use against the Boarisk.

"Alarms don't just malfunction," the other one, another Boarisk grumbled. "There's someone here. I don't know how they got this low, but they're almost to the lift shaft. If they want to find out what we're doing so badly, we can accommodate them by putting them in the work gangs."

The last thing Skylar wanted was to end up in one of their work gangs. But if he and Gal went missing, he didn't doubt that Solaria and Filzbalm would do their best to tear the Boarisk compound apart, and that would be before Professor Aduncus could finally able to get the planetary council to act and move against the Boarisk on the island.

"Tired of dealing with these fools," Gal muttered softly.

"What?" Skylar asked.

Before he got an answer, the pile of boxes toppled over, falling in a single column onto the two Boarisk guards standing on the other side. The boxes landed with loud clangs followed by heavy thuds from their contents shifting. The floor shook with the impacts.

There were brief squeals of terror, and then the room fell silent. Nothing moved. Skylar stood there staring at where the crates had been. They and their heavy contents had made the perfect weights to drop on the guards.

Skylar glared at Gal. "What did you do?"

"Killed two guards," Gal returned smugly. "Don't tell me you wouldn't do it if you had the chance."

Skylar despised the Boarisk and everything they represented, but he had always envisioned standing in front of them and shooting them, or stabbing them with a sword, or even beating them with the cane he'd recovered after he and his friends had watched an Orcan attack one in the Galaxeria. Dropping crates of heavy tools on them didn't feel…right…fair…honest. Honor…Solaria had talked about honorable kills before. That was what was missing from killing the enemy with a surprise attack using bulky equipment.

But there was nothing he could do about it. Gal had made the call without consulting him.

"If we're lucky the next people to come along will just think it was an accident." Gal stepped around the fallen crates. "We just need to not be here when they show up."

"They said something about the lift tubes being not far from here." Skylar tried to push the dead Boarisks out of his head. When they got back together and didn't have to worry about an Orcan reader picking up on their thoughts, he'd talk to Solaria about it and see what her take on it was. He glanced at the spot where a hoof-like hand stuck out, unmoving, under one of the crates. His stomach knotted.

Turning away as quickly as he could, he followed Gal out of the room and into another short hallway. Even though he hadn't been the one to do it, he felt like he'd just killed his first Boarisks…it didn't feel as good as he'd imagined it would. Two beings who'd been chatting just moments earlier were dead. He wondered if he'd have been able to stop Gal if he'd tried, and if he had, would they have been able to subdue the Boarisk, or would they be on their way to the work gang?

Too many questions and none of them good. Skylar pushed them aside. He had to see if he could find out what happened to Teir and then help the slaves escape.

After that he could worry about the moral ramifications of his actions, or lack thereof.

17
Through The Water

THE DOORS to the lift closed, and Skylar's heart pounded hard. A sudden panic came over him. There was no way out of the tube until they reached the bottom or went back to the top. Gal had jammed the camera as they got in. The lift was fairly large, like it was designed to carry a fair number of people, or massive equipment down to the habitat below. The walls of the lift itself and the tube it traveled in were clear, giving them a view of the ocean around them.

Del had told Skylar about all the fish, corals, and plants in the waters of Tursipia, and the bit of diving he'd done with his friends around Aduncus Island had revealed that, but the waters here weren't teeming with life.

"This isn't right," Gal muttered, sounding utterly disgusted. "Where are the fish? Where's the kelp? This area should be full of life and there's nothing."

"You don't have dead zones in the oceans?" Skylar asked, thinking back on how even the frozen tundra of Pantheria still held a lot of different kinds of creatures, most of which Solaria loved to hunt.

Gal glared at Skylar. "No. Never. We are very careful in our stewardship of this world. This section of ocean shouldn't be like this." He growled. "When the council hears about this, it'll be enough for them to place sanctions against the Orcans for allowing the Boarisk to do this."

"Then we have to make sure to get out of this alive," Skylar reminded him. "If we don't get out alive, we can't warn anyone of anything."

"And we will." Gal set his smooth, round chin in a grim look of determination. "They *will* pay for what they have done. I might not have agreed with Click dragging us into this without telling us everything, but now I understand. This must be stopped."

Skylar nodded as they dropped low enough for the light from the surface to fade so they couldn't see out of the tube anymore. The darkness closed in around them and made him shiver. The area seemed to reflect the grim mood that had engulfed Skylar since Gal killed the two Boarisks right before they got on the lift. The mission was pushing them hard.

Although he'd expected to find Hummassans on the island, Skylar hadn't hoped to find ones he knew. It was just supposed to be recon until they'd found the trap door and gone into the island's depths—but even then he figured they'd go down, poke around a bit and then report back. Things were moving fast, and Skylar wasn't sure what to do. The only option he saw was going deeper into the island, getting more evidence and then getting out.

In the distance, it looked like there was a habitat on the ocean floor. Its lights were bright enough to been seen through the darkness. Skylar could make out lights below them as well, but there was darkness between the two clusters of illumination. It didn't look like the two habitats were connected in any way, unless it was through tunnels in the sea floor.

They passed through the upper level of the habitation. The lights were still dim around them, but it wasn't as dark as it had been in the water.

"Still doesn't look like there's any life around us," Gal said. "This is very bad."

"I think you're right." Skylar stepped back from the edge of the lift car as it entered a building of some kind near the center of the habitation.

The lift stopped.

Skylar's heart pounded even harder.

Soft lights came on.

Gal huffed. "I bet these little piggies are afraid of the dark.

"We can hope," Skylar said, trying to sound surer of himself than he was. He didn't know when Del was going to be back with Astara, but he hoped it would be soon so he and Gal could start heading back to the surface, get out of the building and off the island.

The lift door opened.

Skylar was surprised there wasn't anyone standing there with a gun pointed at them. Instead there was another hall, much like the one on the island, thousands of feet above them. It didn't make him feel any better about their situation.

18
An Unexpected Secret

SKYLAR WAS doing his best not to get frustrated despite beginning to think that most of the detailed information they were looking for was somewhere up on the island above them. They'd found numerous rooms with crates both empty and full, although they hadn't been able to get any more of them open like they had the boxes of engine parts. Gal pronounced them space-worthy. It made Skylar wonder if the containers were full of the same things the one Del and the others had made off with.

"We're not getting anywhere," Gal grumbled as they entered another room full of crates.

"I'm with you there." Skylar wondered if it was time to try scanning again to give them a direction to go in. He'd been hesitant to use his powers too much after almost being discovered by the Orcan reader in the locker room. He took a slow breath and started to open his mind.

"Skylar." Professor Aduncus' thoughts brushed his. *"Can you hear me?"*

"Professor." Skylar jumped slightly, then hoped any of the other telepaths in the area weren't hearing their exchange. *"Gal and I are in the habitat below the island. There are Orcans working with the Boarisk."*

"Have you run into trouble?" Aduncus asked, sounding far away.

"So far we've been able to avoid it, just barely. We've found slaves, and lots and lots of cargo boxes,

some of them filled with internal combustion engine parts." Skylar leaned against the stack of crates. "Gal, Professor Aduncus is checking on us. Can you watch out for any surprises for a moment?"

"Sure. I've got the door covered," Gal replied.

"Combustion engines were outlawed centuries ago. Are they working, or just antiques?" The professor sounded confused by the announcement.

"Look new, or at least they do to us. Has Del gotten the container his team made off with back to you yet?"

"Yes. Astara is one of the fastest ships on the planet. You have all done an amazing job modding her." There was a note of pride in Aduncus' mental voice.

"What was in it?" Skylar didn't want to keep their connection open too long for fear of being detected. Even though his link was Aduncus was strong due to months of training to use his telepathy, they had no idea how powerful the Orcans were, or if they had any other readers, possibly among the slaves.

"Oscenite, some of the purest ever recorded."

Skylar tried to remember where he'd heard of oscenite before. "Gal, what's oscenite?"

"It's a mineral used on starships, space stations, and in spacesuits for oxygen purification. It's fairly rare. Why?"

"It's what they're mining here." Skylar said. *"Wait, Gal says it's rare. So it's valuable?"*

"Very," the professor replied. *"One of the most valuable minerals in the universe right now. There are known deposits on Tursipia, but mining it here is very deep and makes the plates unstable, so we don't dig it on our planet."*

"The Orcans and Boarisk don't care about the planet, Professor." Skylar glared at the filled crates around him, wishing there was some way other than opening one to see if there was really more oscenite in

them. But the crate Del took back was probably proof enough.

"I've called the planetary council together. We're going to have a conference call shortly. There will be Orcan delegates in attendance. Hopefully we can get something worked out. Del and the others are on their way to retrieve you, Gal, Solaria, and Filzbalm."

A sharp pain hit Skylar. It felt like Solaria was using his skull as a scratching post. He grabbed his head and dropped to his knees.

Gal knelt next to him. "Skylar? Man, what's wrong?"

Skylar tried to pull his thoughts together enough to form words, but he couldn't. His head hurt too much. He'd been relying on Professor Aduncus to shield their connection. Someone, a powerful reader, had hit him hard, breaking his communication with the professor. If the Boarisk and Orcans had a reader that powerful, they had to know where Skylar and Gal were.

Skylar struggled to his feet. "Got to get out of here." The room full of crates spun around him, and he leaned on Gal as he fought to keep his balance.

"They hit you, didn't they?" Gal said, wrapping an arm around Skylar's waist.

"Hard. Need to move." The pain eased, second by second, but Skylar knew he had just become a liability to them getting out of the habitation and up to the island, where Astara would be picking them up shortly.

"Skylar?" Filzbalm's thoughts hit him hard.

Skylar stumbled and wished he could sit down. *"Filzbalm. I'm trying to head back. Been attacked by a reader. Stay quiet. Stay hidden. We're coming."*

There was a flash of anger from the Solar Drake, but no more words. That was good. Skylar wasn't sure he could handle mind to mind communications until his brain cleared from the attack.

They made it to the door.

"Lean against the wall," Gal said as he slowly opened the door to peer out.

Skylar wasn't about to argue. He eased his head back until it was against the smooth metal wall. He wanted to slide down the wall until he could sit and go to sleep. Being unconscious always helped after a reader-caused headache.

"We look clear for the moment." Gal eased himself under Skylar's arm again. "Back to the lift?"

"Yeah, that's good." Skylar forced the words out. Even thinking hurt. He needed rest, but they weren't going to get that until they got off the island.

Gal started off down the hallway. Skylar did his best to keep up and not pull Gal down too far. They made it past a couple of doors, then the sound of footsteps rushing toward them pulled them up short.

"In there." Skylar pointed weakly toward the door. It was a room full of crates that they'd already been in, but it would get them out of the hallway.

"Okay." Gal opened the door and got them in.

"This just went from boring to busy," Skylar muttered as he leaned against the wall.

"Right," Gal agreed, putting his ear against the door. "We're going to need a bit of luck to get out of here, aren't we?"

"Looking like it," Skylar said. "Can you see if there might be another door in this room? We haven't checked for that." As he said that, he realized they'd been more than a little sloppy in their search. But they weren't spies, or action heroes. He was a student. Gal…he didn't know exactly what Gal was, other than a friend of Click's. They also weren't hunters like Solaria. She would've been a lot more thorough in investigating things. He wished his head didn't hurt so much so he could risk reaching out and getting her advice. He hated being cut off from his friends. During his time at Stars' End, he'd started taking it for granted that they would always be there for him, even if only mentally.

"I've got another door," Gal said from a few feet away.

Skylar opened his eyes, not having realized he'd closed them in hopes of getting his head to stop hurting. At least all the rooms and halls in the habitat were lit. That was an improvement over the ones on the island.

Skylar forced himself upright. "Let's see if we can go that way."

Gal helped steady Skylar. "Maybe there's a hatch or something we can use to escape that way. It looks like it runs along the dome's outer wall."

"That's a long way up," Skylar said. "I don't know about Tursiops, but Humans aren't designed for long exposure to deep water. I bet we're several hundred feet down."

Gal chuckled. "Try several thousand. The ocean floor in this part of the world is nearly fifty thousand feet down. Even we can't survive at this depth for very long. I might be able to swim to the surface, but it would be questionable."

"Then we need to either get back to the lift, or find an escape pod of some kind. You'd think something like this would have such a thing." Skylar stumbled again as they left the storage room and entered another hall.

The new curving hall had a clear wall opposite them. It looked out onto the dead ocean around the habitat. The lights from the dome only reached a few hundred feet at most—then murky darkness, that looked totally different from the welcoming depths of space, greeted them. A chill went through Skylar. He didn't want to find himself out in that dark water. He'd be dead, and so would Filzbalm back up on the island above them.

"Let's head back in the direction of the lifts," Gal said, steering them toward the right.

A telepathic probe passed over them. Skylar clung to Gal, somehow managing to keep his feet as the pain in his head renewed.

"They're looking for us," Skylar forced out through gritted teeth. He was going to practice his shielding with every fiber of his being. If they managed to get out of the habitat, up to the island and back to Astara, he would get his shielding to the point that nobody was going to be able to get through his protections ever again.

"Yeah, and not subtly," Gal muttered. "Even I felt that, and I'm not a reader. Something's majorly wrong with these people."

"Yeah, you could say that." Skylar realized as they stumbled along that that was the key to the assaults he'd felt. They were like being hit with a club. They lacked any kind of finesse. Whoever was hitting them either hadn't had much training, didn't care what they were doing, or liked inflicting pain on other people. Since they were dealing with Boarisk and Orcans, the last option didn't surprise him. They were both brutish races.

Footfalls came from the direction they were heading. They stopped.

"Now what?" Gal muttered.

"Back the way we came," Skylar suggested. They hadn't passed any intersections, ladders, or lifts. Back was their only option and hope the undulating corridors gave them some cover, unless Gal wanted to fight it out with whoever was coming toward them. Skylar didn't think he would be much use to Gal in a fight with his head pounding the way it was.

Gal turned them around and they headed back a little faster than they'd been moving. Each step jarred more pain thought Skylar's head. He'd almost found a tolerable way of walking with the slower pace, but hurrying was torturous. The constant twists and turns in the corridors made it hard for him to keep track of their direction, and the pounding in his head left him completely disoriented, hardly knowing which way was up.

They made it to a spot where their dome intersected with the next dome over. More footfalls rang out on the tile floor.

"This way." Gal pulled Skylar along the corridor into the next dome. "Maybe they won't think we went this far."

"Yeah, hopefully." Skylar was in so much pain he couldn't really care about much beyond getting somewhere he could lie down and wait until he felt better. Bile rose in his throat and with each step, he struggled to keep from throwing up from the agony in his skull.

Gal stopped at a door and opened it. "I think it's clear. It's at least dark."

"Okay," Skylar numbly agreed. If they could stop moving, he might be able to get the pain to recede with some of the professor's meditation techniques.

Gal closed the door. The room was indeed dark. Skylar couldn't even see Gal, whom he still had an arm wrapped around him.

He clicked on his palmlight and blinked against the brightness. Slowly he panned the light over their surroundings. They were in an office of some kind. A couple of desks sat near clear poly walls looking out into another room. The other room was so large the light couldn't reach to the far side. There were a number of what looked like hospital beds and some equipment Skylar didn't recognize. The beds were all unoccupied, and no one was visible anywhere in the limited light.

"Sit down." Gal angled Skylar toward one of the chairs at a desk. "Maybe we can hang out in here for a little while, or at least until that reader scans for us again."

Skylar leaned his head back against the chair's headrest. "That's a good idea." He was thankful it was a tall backed chair and not like some of the short ones in the cafeteria on Stars' End. The headrest was the right height to support his neck and let him relax a little bit.

"Stay there," Gal said. "Let me have the palmlight and I'll see what I can find over here."

"Are you good with computers?" Skylar asked as he pulled the light's strap free of his hand and relinquished it to Gal. If Del or Melody had been there, they could've gotten into the computers quickly. Astara would've already been downloading everything they contained into her memory banks for analysis.

"Decent," Gal mumbled as he took another chair and turned on the system there. "Let's just hope they can't read the power spike and come running."

"I hope so." Skylar closed his eyes and tried to relax and make the throbbing in his head stop. He wasn't great at meditation but wasn't up for even the simplest katas, the smooth, almost dance-like movements Professor Aduncus had taught him as a way to relax and access his gifts.

The longer they were in the room, the more relaxed Skylar became and the less his head pounded.

"Hey, this isn't good," Gal said.

Skylar opened his eyes. "What did you find?"

"We need to get this data to the Professor and the council," Gal said. "They're doing experiments here. In addition to mining oscenite, they're trying to artificially give people psychic gifts."

"Gene manipulation is illegal." Skylar didn't think he was up to standing yet, so he slid his chair over to the terminal Gal was working on. The display was projected on the window between the two rooms. There was a lot of data there. Skylar wasn't sure he followed most of it.

"Right, and so is having an island out here with a habitat on the ocean floor," Gal added as he opened a drawer and rummaged around in it.

"Yeah, the bad guys never really care about the laws, do they?" Skylar leaned toward the display and started scrolling through data with flicks of his hand. He tried to wrap his pained mind around what he was seeing, but it didn't make much sense. They had to get it out of the computer and back to Del and the professor.

"Here we go." Gal pulled out a small clear crystal. "Let's get this data and run." He put the crystal in the data clip, an interface between the computer and the crystals that were occasionally used for storage. "The crystal isn't large enough for everything, so we'll get enough to give us the proof we need and get out of here."

Gal paused Skylar's scrolling and started moving data from the computer to the crystal.

"This is going to take a couple of minutes." Gal leaned back in his chair and handed the palmlight back to Skylar.

Lights flashed in the other room, and a claxon rang out.

The sound hit Skylar hard. He rocked to the side as his nausea returned, and emptied the contents of his stomach onto the floor beside his chair.

"We don't have a couple of minutes." Gal yanked the crystal out of the clip. "Fifty percent will have to do."

Skylar struggled to his feet, wishing there was somewhere they could hide long enough for the claxons to stop so they could escape when everything returned to normal.

With Gal supporting Skylar, they made it back out into the hall. People were rushing out from the other rooms along the corridor. There were too many people.

They were a mix different species and many sexes, most confused and scared.

The emotions hit Skylar nearly as hard as the reader's attacks had. He wanted to stop where he was and curl up into a ball, hoping it would all just go away. Gal was focused on getting them out though, and that focus helped Skylar push back at the emotions of the other people around them.

"That's them. Stop them!" someone shouted behind them.

Skylar knew who they were talking about. Ahead of them, people plastered themselves to the walls and a group of guards appeared farther down the corridor.

"I think I can stop their bullets and blaster beams, but we can only hold out so long," Gal said. "We need to get out of here."

"Right." Skylar mumbled. His palm itched where the shard of the Crystal Claw was. He might be able to do something, but it would be risky, and the way his head was hurting he wouldn't be overly focused.

The first blast came at them. Gal blocked it.

"Hang on." Skylar focused on the crystal. It helped push the pain in his head away. The shard surged and Skylar was suddenly linked with Gal. The mover's powers were at his command. Skylar reached out to other minds, trying to find all the power he could. Maybe he could put everyone to sleep. More power than he expected was available to him. He tapped into it.

"Solaria, Filzbalm, lend me a hand here," he called out to the others on the island.

"I've got the pain," Filzbalm said. For the first time since the initial attack, mental contact didn't hurt.

"What do you need?" Solaria sounded eager for a fight.

"Help Gal protect us from the guards while I tap into the other psychics in here with us."

"On it." Solaria easily used their gestalt to link in with Gal. *"We movers gotta move."*

"Thanks," Gal said as another round of blast hit them.

Skylar found the power he was looking for, but like the attacks, it was raw, tainted, and unfocused. He did his best to draw it and feed it to Gal and Solaria as he tried to remember how to put people to sleep with his mind.

Then he mentally touched something familiar.

19
Through Fire And Water

THE MIND Skylar touched felt like a familiar old shoe. He struggled to understand. Power flowed from that mind, power he could tap into, but it was strange power. There was someone he knew rushing toward him. But there was so much going on.

He poured power into Gal. Solaria and Filzbalm added their own to the effort. Gal crafted a shield around them strong enough to block most blasts, but it didn't help them get out of the mess they were in.

"Skylar, you're going to have to move, go somewhere," Solaria said.

"Working on it." Skylar harnessed the power of the minds around him and started pushing back, trying remember how to put people to sleep without hurting them. There was so much he needed to learn more about.

"Let me." Filzbalm said. The Solar Drake took control of Skylar's mind, riding hard over the gestalt between them and Gal. He pushed Skylar's powers out, brushing against every mind he could and dropping them in their tracks.

"The Orcans and the others are falling," Gal said. *"But it's not affecting the Boarisk."*

"Their minds are safe with their lack of gifts," Filzbalm said. *"There are reasons they aren't allowed on Armstrong's Ring."* The anger hitting Skylar from the Solar Drake was nearly equal to his own hatred for the swine.

Skylar let Filzbalm handle the more delicate mental work. With their gestalt stopping the pain from the attack he suffered, Skylar eased a little of his power to contacting the mind he'd brushed against. Why was it familiar? He couldn't think of anyone who would've been that strong that should be in the habitat with them.

"*Who are you?*" Skylar asked.

"*Skylar? You sound and feel like Skylar Mars, but that's not possible. You're dead.*" Confusion came through his weak connection with the other mind. "*This has to be some kind of illusion.*"

Dead? There was only one person who would think Skylar was dead, and it made sense, but not the power of the mind. "*Teir? Oh God. Teir. Your mother said you were here somewhere. I didn't know you were psychic.*"

"*This can't be you,*" Teir replied. "*It has to be another one of their tricks. They've been trying to break me, and now they're using you to do that. I won't let them.*"

A wall of flame erupted between Skylar and Teir.

"*Skylar, I can't protect you and keep putting minds to sleep,*" Filzbalm shouted. "*You've got to push back against the flames.*"

Understanding, Skylar used his own reader gifts to push against the flames and soothe them away. "*Teir, it is me. I'm not an illusion. You've got to listen to me. We're trying to save you and the other slaves here in the habitat and on the island.*"

In the mindscape, Teir appeared on the other side of the flames. He looked a lot like Skylar remembered, but he had aged in the year they'd been apart. Where Skylar had grown naturally, taller, broader, quickly becoming the man he was going to be, Teir had shriveled—he was almost an old man, bent and stooped, even his hair was nearly white, something only the oldest of Hummassans ever got.

"Teir, please, you have to believe me." Skylar reached out a mental hand to him. *"I'm here to save you. Your mother sent me."*

Teir looked up, his yellow eyes filled with pain and fear. *"My mother. They got her too. They killed my father and brothers."*

The second bit was news to Skylar, but he just nodded and inched closer. *"I know. I saw Taglia up on the island, in the slave quarters. She would've come with us, but the slave bracelets keep her there."*

Nodding Teir looked at his wrist, there were slave bracelets there too. "They seek to bind us. They've done a good job of it."

Skylar took Teir's hands. *"I know. We're going to break those bonds."* Power flowed between them. It was like Teir had suddenly tapped into their group power source and drew energy from the gestalt. The flames grew again, seeming to come out of Teir and cover him from head to toe, but they didn't burn Skylar.

"It's about time they see what they've created." The slave bands liquified in the heat. Teir screamed in pain.

Skylar instinctively wrapped Teir in a protective psychic shield.

"He's off the charts," Solaria said. *"Skylar, help him."*

"Something just exploded near us," Gal said. *"I blocked it, but just barely."* A surge of fear boiled out of Gal. *"But it cracked the dome. Skylar, we've got to get out of here."*

"Not without Teir." Skylar focused his attention on his oldest friend. *"Come on Teir. Can you get to us? We've got to go. The dome just cracked. We're in the hallway next to the outside of the habitat."*

The pull of power from Teir stopped. He smiled weakly. *"Maybe. I'll try."* He paused, then hugged

Skylar. *"Thank you. Even if the ocean kills us now, you've freed me."*

Then he was gone.

"Skylar, there's only so much we can do about the dome cracking," Gal said. *"Even our gestalt isn't strong enough to hold it together. We need to go."*

"Go where?" Skylar asked. *"It's not like either you or Solaria can teleport us out of here."* He had no idea what they were going to be able to do. If the dome cracked they were going to drown—even if they made it up to the lift, their chances of survival were minimal. They needed a miracle.

The blasts hitting Gal's shield stopped. Skylar stopped focusing all his attention on the mental link between them and let himself focus on the corridor they stood in. Around them, Orcans and other people lay unconscious—there were even a couple of Boarisk down. Skylar couldn't tell if they were asleep or had somehow been injured in the guards' attempts to break through Gal's shield. Flames danced along the hallway from a room a few doors down. They seemed to be trying to reach the crack in the dome that was bulging inward. The pressure from the ocean floor was trying to equalize with the pressure inside the habitat.

"Escape pods," Skylar said. "Let's find the escape pods. I wish we had floorplans."

"We're working on that," Del said, suddenly part of their shared mind. *"Astara is close enough that she's trying to access their computer system through the backdoor she left when we discovered the island."*

"Del! You're back." A surge of hope filled Skylar. With Del, Solaria and Filzbalm they just might be able to think of something.

"We've got movement, Skylar." Gal pulled Skylar's attention back to the hallway.

From the room where the flames danced, a frail red-skinned figure entered the hallway. Like it had been in the mindscape, Teir's hair was white. He moved like he wasn't used to walking, and each step seemed painful.

"Teir." Skylar's heart sank. He'd hoped Teir's appearance had been a product of his mental image of himself, but it hadn't been. If anything he looked worse in the physical world than he had in the mental one. "Gal, we've got to get to him."

"The way that fire's growing, I'm not sure that's a good idea," Gal objected. "At least the guards have all fled, probably to escape pods." Gal dropped his shield. The pull on Skylar's powers instantly backed off.

"Skylar, the guards from the island are all running into different buildings," Solaria announced.

"They're probably trying to get down here to help out before the place implodes." Skylar rushed away from Gal toward Teir. "It's not going to do any good. There's too much damage." He grabbed Teir and hugged him. "Teir. You're safe now."

"Skylar, I've got an escape pod near you," Del said.

"Skylar. It's really you." Teir hugged him back and started crying. "I can't believe it."

"I'm here."

Something wet splashed Skylar's cheek.

"Skylar, hold on!" Gal shouted.

The ripple of telekinetic power across his skin let Skylar know Gal was doing something. Then the three of them were thrown off their feet. Skylar braced himself, trying to turn slightly so he'd be the one to hit the wall and not Teir.

He never hit the wall, but they were tossed around.

"Skylar, Gal, hold on, we're trying to help," Solaria said. *"Filzbalm, what's happening?"*

Through their gestalt, they ripped power out of Skylar. He was used to being the one pulling energy from the others and directing it. The crystal in his hand burned as the power flowed contrary to what they were used to. Someone screamed. Skylar couldn't tell if it was Gal or Teir.

"The dome's collapsing," Del said instead of Filzbalm. *"They're being sucked out into the ocean. It's too deep. They'll never survive."*

"Let me try to teleport them." Solaria sounded frantic.

Skylar was tossed about in Gal's protective sphere. He bounced into Teir and Gal alternatively. He couldn't think of anything to help save them, but at that moment, he just wanted the bouncing to stop.

"We don't have that kind of power," Del said.

"Let me see if I can get help," Filzbalm said.

The conversation was washed out of reach as they continued to roll away from the dome. Skylar was gasping for breath by the time the energy bubble finally came to a stop.

"Slow it down," Gal whispered.

"What?" Skylar muttered, his words came out course from his throat.

"Your breathing, slow it down," Gal replied softly. "We've only got a little bit of air in here, and we don't want to use it up too quickly."

Skylar almost held his breath. It was like being in space without the stars. They had a limited supply of air and every breath they took used it up faster and faster.

They'd escaped the Boarisk habitat, but if Gal or their friends couldn't get them to the surface in time, they were going to drown.

20
Swimming With The Fishes

SKYLAR FORCED himself to breathe as shallowly as possible. Their best hope was Gal being able to move the sphere they were in up to the surface. He, Gal, and Teir were sitting on the floor of the sphere, although it was somewhat flattened out where they were. He knew from Solaria that movers could make their telekinetic fields any shape, but spheres were almost a default for them. She said it was just easier due to the equal distribution of energy or something like that.

"We need more power," Solaria said. *"If Professor Ruff was here, maybe we could get enough mover energy together to pop you guys up here."*

"But he's not," Del replied. *"And you and Leonada are the only ones taking classes from him, so there's not a strong enough link to pull him into our group mind. Maybe Grandfather could help with that. I wish he or Yul had come back with us."*

"I do too," Skylar said.

"Astara might be able to reach you. She says she's designed to withstand oceans as well as space and atmospheres," Del said. *"Instead of landing, we're heading down."*

"Looks like we've got more problems down here." Gal pointed to the side of the bubble that was away from the habitat.

A dozen large fish were swimming toward them. Each one of them held some kind of glowing staff.

"What are they?" Skylar had never seen anything like them before.

"Resmordians," Gal said. "They look really upset."

"Del, we've got Resmordians coming in on us." Skylar wasn't sure if there was anything Del could do, but he hoped there would be. He didn't want to end up dead in the ocean.

"I'll let Grandfather know." Then Del was gone from their link.

The fishmen swam around the sphere in what appeared to be a very agitated fashion.

Next to Skylar, Teir stirred. "What's going on?"

"Short answer—we're in a telekinetic bubble at the bottom of a very deep ocean and we're surrounded by upset fishmen," Skylar said.

Teir rubbed his head. "I've never tried anything powerful enough to knock myself out before." He looked at his wrists. "I got rid of the slave bracelets. I shouldn't have been able to do that, or at least that's what they told us."

"We might've lent a little help," Skylar said. "But without more help, we're going to die real soon."

"We're on our way down," Del said. *"Hang on."*

The Resmordians outside the sphere began swimming in a huge circle.

"I don't think this is good," Gal said.

"Del, the Resmordians are up to something." Skylar tried to stay calm as water outside their protective shelter started to glow an eerie blue.

The telekinetic orb protecting them shook.

Gal grabbed his head. "Definitely not good. That's a lot of pressure they're applying to our protections."

"We're almost there," Del said.

"Hurry." Skylar didn't bother trying to keep the fear from his mind. He didn't know how much longer Gal

could hold out, even with Skylar and the others feeding him power.

The water around them blazed a brilliant, blinding blue. Gal's protective sphere shook violently, and everything fell away. Skylar reached out for the others, but their gestalt was ripped apart. Their shouts filled his head. Filzbalm's anger was tangible. For just a second, he though the Solar Drake was with him.

Then it all changed. Everything got quiet. Lights blinded him, driving him into darkness.

"COME ON, Skylar." Gal shook him slightly. "You need to wake up. I can't contact the others with you asleep."

Skylar forced his eyes opened and stared at Gal. "What happened?"

Gal looked as confused as Skylar felt. Teir lay unconscious a few feet away.

"We've been moved," Gal said. "I don't know where. I mean, I think we're still on Tursipia, but beyond that, I can't tell. Well, and that we are under water."

Skylar sighed. That didn't really help much. He closed his eyes and reached out to his friends. The crystal in his palm burned, but the only minds he could touch were Gal and Teir. He couldn't even feel Filzbalm. It made him wonder if they weren't being blocked somehow. Not even Professor Aduncus could keep him from reaching Filzbalm.

He opened his eyes and shook his head. "There must be some kind of dampening field or something. I can't reach anyone." When he'd been wearing a dampening bracelet, during the time he was learning to control his reader powers, he'd been cut off from everyone, but sitting there in…wherever they were…it was strange not feeling at least Filzbalm in the back of his mind.

He glanced around, but the room was totally nondescript. Just walls, floor and ceiling. No chairs, no desks, no carpeting…nothing but a door behind Gal. "So other than under the water, any idea where we're at?"

Gal shook his head. "I haven't seen anyone since I came to. Any clue what they did to us? If I had to guess, I'd say some kind of teleportation, but I don't understand the glowing staves." He stood and paced away from Skylar. "It reminded me of some kind of stargate, but that doesn't make any sense at all."

"I know, I've never heard of anything like that," Skylar said, but he knew there were a lot of things in the universe he had never heard of. He wasn't sure how much energy it would take to create a stargate, even a small one, to transport three people in a telekinetic bubble across a planet. It didn't seem like a economic use of power.

"More weirdness in existence," Teir muttered as he sat up next to Skylar. "That's been my life over the past year."

"I guess that describes mine too," Skylar agreed.

"Well, the door's locked," Gal announced with a frown as he turned from the door and stared at them.

Skylar shrugged. Although he'd never been taken captive in real life, there had been a few times when he and Teir had been playing their favorite video game, Galactic Explorers, and had ended up captives in a hostile situation. "Then we wait and see what they want with us. I'm sure the minute we disappeared, Del alerted Professor Aduncus. They know it was the Resmordians that made us vanish. The professor will contact the planetary council, and they'll work through diplomatic channels to get us back."

Gal laughed. "If we're not dead by then. I know you're not from Tursipia, but things don't always work that way here."

"Is that where we are, Tursipia?" Teir asked. "I knew we were underwater, but didn't know where."

Skylar nodded. "I'm in school here. It's where some Stars' End students ended up after the space station was destroyed by the AI Armada."

Teir shook his head. "Sorry, I have no clue what you're talking about."

Skylar sighed as he stood. "My fault. A lot has happened since I was rescued on Hummassa. I guess we have time now—I can fill you in, then you can tell me about your journey." Pacing the small room made it easier to get his tale out, and the telling of it took longer than Skylar had anticipated. Overall, it had been the most exciting year of his life. Telling it to Teir made it all sound very fantastic and amazing, although only certain parts had hit him that way as he'd experienced them firsthand.

"Wow, you got the good stuff," Teir said. "I wasn't so lucky." He closed his eyes for a moment.

It struck Skylar that he couldn't pick up any kind of emotion from Teir as he prepared to bring Skylar up to date. They were definitely in a room with some kind of dampening field to block their psychic abilities. Since they weren't a humanoid species, it was odd that the Resmordians would have the tech to do that.

Sure, he knew other non-humanoids who used humanoid tech, but if the Resmordians were actually the ancient, original species ofTursipia, he'd expected them to be primitives for some reason. When they'd swam toward them carrying the staves, they'd looked like the ancient cave humans depicted in history lessons. But if they were sharing the world with the Tursiops and the Orcans, they had to have some ability to maintain equal footing or they'd have been wiped out when the planet was colonized.

21
Teir's Tale

SKYLAR WAITED patiently for his friend to speak, until Teir heaved a heavy, sad sigh., and then Teir launched into his story. "We weren't lucky enough to be saved after the Boarisk attack back home. I remember running out of the house seconds after the fire started. Mom, Dad, and my brothers were with me. We did what we could to put out the fire, trying to save the house. With most of the other houses around us also going up in flames, and people trying to save their property, there wasn't enough water to go around. Even when they started pumping salt water into the main system, we couldn't get enough to do any good.

"Dad was just giving up on the house when the first transport landed. Since none of us had actually seen who attacked the houses, we all went racing to the rescue." Teir shook his head. "If we'd known what, or who we were rushing toward, we'd have run into the forest. I don't know, but I bet that's why the Boarisk spend so much time shooting things up when they collect slaves, so they don't actually have to round up the healthy—we just hurried out to their ships expecting them to be help. If we get out of this, I want to let everyone on the less developed worlds know their tricks. I want to help save people."

Skylar understood all too well. After what he'd witnessed on Hummassa and other places, and after working with Solaria's uncle Phil, he wanted to find ways to help people too. Most of the species in the universe needed people to watch out for them when there were maurading people like the Boarisk, or even during natural disasters—who better than the psychics who had the power to help?

"I'm not sure what they did to us as we ran into the ships; maybe it was gas, maybe it was electricity. It all happened so fast. One second we were going up the ramp, and the next thing I knew I was waking up on a deep-space transport. They'd already put the slave cuffs on us. One of the guys, an old fisherman from somewhere nearby…I remember him from the markets when Mom would take us with her. You probably remember him too, he was the only one there who had white hair and one of his eyes was missing."

"Yeah," Skylar said. "I remember him. He normally had freshwater clams because he said deep-sea fishing and clamming were too dangerous. It was how he lost his eye. I don't remember his name though."

Teir pursed his lips and nodded solemnly. "I feel bad that I don't either."

"Guys, I wouldn't talk about fishermen around here." Gal glanced around nervously. "Some of the Resmordians can be touchy about that subject. If they're listening it might not be a good thing."

Teir nodded, then continued talking. "He pulled at his bracelets. The Boarisks guarding us started laughing. If I never hear another Boarisk laugh, I can die happy. They just laughed and laughed until the bracelets activated and shocked him. The first shock knocked him down, but he kept tugging at them, trying to get them off. He was cussing the Boarisks the whole time. The second shock knocked him unconscious. That did stop him. The third shock killed him. We all learned then not to mess with the bracelets.

"After a month or so on the transport, I think we went through some stargates, but I'm not sure. I think they were trying to confuse us, make us feel lost in space."

"Once you realize what you're doing, you can tell when you're going through a stargate," Skylar interrupted. "Or at least I can. It's really awesome." He wondered if he was right that the Resmordians had created a mini stargate of some kind. The feeling immediately before he passed out had felt a bit like a stargate transferring them across a vast distance.

"Most people can't tell the difference between regular space travel and going through a gate, unless you happen to be in the cockpit, or at a window where you can see the event horizon of the wormhole," Gal said.

"I guess it really doesn't matter," Teir said. "I mean. I'm here, on Tursipia. So, we must've gone through at least one gate jump."

"And you weren't in the Hummassa system when Intergal Rescue arrived," Skylar added. "So they left really quickly."

"Once we woke up with the bracelets on, things didn't go so quickly," Teir continued. "We were in that ship for a month or more. The Boarisks would come through our hold from time to time and pick certain people to leave. Normally it was the young and pretty ones. They didn't care what species. At one point we got more prisoners—they were Pawlieans. After they recovered from their capture, they explained they were from an outpost world in their system.

"But it was during that time that Dad and my brothers died. They were defending Mom and me from the Boarisks. Some of the guards like to take advantage of our slavery, demanding we do what they tell us to, even if we didn't want to." Teir stared at the floor and clenched his fists. It was obvious he wanted to give the pigs payback for what they'd done to his family and friends.

It was a feeling Skylar understood well.

"I don't know who was worse off," Teir went on after a moment. "Them or me. I have the power to make them pay, but I've undergone a lot to get it. Maybe it would've been better if I'd been brave enough to act with Dad, Takaro, and Telemier. Sure, I'd have died with them, but…"

Skylar put a hand on Teir's shoulder and shook his head. "But you would've left your mother alone. She's still alive because you were there to be with her."

"Not for a while now." Teir stared at his hands, then looked up at Skylar. "Not since they came and took me away for their experiments. That wasn't until we'd been here for a couple of months working in the mines. They worked us until we dropped, barely giving us enough food and water to keep going, but I think we were all determined to continue on, in hopes of escaping and giving the Boarisks what they deserved."

"We'll make sure they get what's coming to them," Gal said. "Once we get out of here, we'll use the Aduncus' connections in the council to get the slaves free and shut the Boarisks down for good, at least here on Tursipia—them and the Orcans too."

"Don't forget the humans," Teir added. "Humans were in on this too. I think they might've been the ones ultimately in charge. At least that's what I saw when they were around. The Boarisk and the…Orcans? Is that what you called the big black and white ones that looked a bit like you do?"

Gal jerked back like he'd been hit and glared at Teir. "Tursiops don't look like Orcans. I mean, we might have skin that is similar texture, but they're Orcans. Nothing like us."

"Maybe it's just something outsiders see," Teir said.

"But wait a minute, there were humans here? In the Boarisk habitat?" After everything Skylar had learned since leaving Hummassa, he wasn't surprised that his people were involved in illegal gene manipulation. The Central Galactic Council had a lot of things in their history they weren't very forthcoming about. The odds were really good either that they, or one of the many corporations that controlled them, had their fingers in a large number of illegal things, including gene manipulation.

Playing around with the genes of species, or even individuals, was one of the high crimes of the Central Galatic Council. No one had explained why it was so, but with the things Skylar had discovered since leaving Hummassa, there was a lot of evidence that tampering with the human genome had been a big thing when humans had been exploring the universe, but had since been shut down. It wasn't overly surprising that the Boarisk and Orcans were doing what they could to change the genes of other species. Maybe the Boarisk were trying to find a way to give their race psychic abilities. Since they'd awakened them in Teir, that was a distinct possibility. Skylar wanted desperately to get back to Astara so he could talk to Del and the others about it and see what they thought.

"Several of them," Teir confirmed. "They seemed to be in charge of the testing rooms. That's where they took those of us they thought might have dormant genes for psychic skills, genes they were trying to awaken."

Skylar shook his head, wishing Del was there to help him figure out things. "But Hummassans aren't prone to psi skills. There's a list of races that either don't have them, like Boarisks, or only display them under extreme duress…" He drew out the last word as he realized what had caused his oldest friend to appear to age as badly as he had. They'd been torturing him to get his powers to manifest. Skylar's own gifts had first activated during times of stress, his feeler gift during the attack on Hummassa, and his reader gift during an unpleasant discussion with Ms. Grissom, then the head counselor at Stars' End Academy.

Teir nodded and looked like he understood Skylar's reaction. "Yes, they induced extreme duress. I suppose I should consider myself lucky that they didn't involve my mother in that exercise. Some of the children who didn't respond to their own…ah…stimulation were forced to watch as their parents were tortured until they lashed out with their fledgling powers."

Skylar's hatred for the Boarisk grew.

"The Orcans and pigs are monsters," Gal hissed. "Our gifts are supposed to grow naturally or not at all."

Before any of them could say anything more, the door opened. No one came in, and it looked like there was water just on the other side of the threshold. Beyond that, one of the Resmordians swam just outside the opening. It looked like open ocean behind it.

"You have all recovered from your transport here." The fishman's voice rang in Skylar's head. It felt loud and uncomfortable as it rolled through his skull. From the look on Gal and Teir's faces, it was hitting them hard as well.

Skylar stepped to the doorway. *"Yes. We have. Where are we?"* He thought about responding verbally, but since the Resmordian was obviously a reader, it made sense to use his mind instead.

"Far from where you started." The reply included an image of the dead ocean around the Boarisk habitat, followed by a coral sea teaming with various forms of aquatic life.

The pictures that came with the words were reminiscent of talking with the cows back on Stars' End, except the verbal part of the communication was more complex than cows could muster. The reef could've been anywhere on Tursipia, other than the dead zone around the Boarisk island. It didn't help Skylar know where he was. And, although he could communicate with the Resmordian, he still couldn't feel Filzbalm or any of his friends.

"Why did you take us from the dead ocean?" Skylar hoped he didn't sound too angry. Although he didn't know how the Resmordians were keeping the water from their room, he didn't want to upset them and have the place flooded.

"We've been waiting for an opportunity to ask you why you have killed the ocean there. Why have you violated our waters and broken our treaty?" There was an accompanying image of a group of Humans and Tursiops on a beach conferring with several Resmordians in the water beyond them. It looked very official.

"We're not the ones who killed that section of ocean," Skylar replied. *"It was the Boarisk and the Orcans."* He pictured basic members of both races in his mind.

The Resmordian stopped its easy undulating swimming and froze in the water. *"You speak the truth as you understand it, but we have been watching that island for a long time—since the ocean there first started to fail, when the ones we share the water with came to us begging for help and sanctuary from the destruction. There are many on the island and in the dome that protects them from our waters, the dome which leaks poison into the water."* The pictures changed quickly, showing the various species Skylar had seen among the slaves and the Boarisk and Orcans. There were even a few humans in white lab coats. Images of fish large and small came rushing at him. Then there was the sight of dark waste curling out of the domes and into the waters around them. There was more than a little anger accompanying the scenes that flashed in Skylar's head.

"Okay, that's bad." Skylar tried to push a feeling of despair out as he spoke. *"That is just one of the reasons why we fight to get the Boarisk and their allies out of your waters and off this planet."* He wished Professor Aduncus was there to negotiate with the Resmordians. He had no idea what he was doing, or if he was saying the right thing to get them out of the situation without making things worse.

"So, you fight against the pillagers." The Resmordian resumed his undulating motion. Lights flickered off his silvery scales, and Skylar wondered if they were close to the surface, or if not, where the light was coming from.

"Yes." Instead of telling him everything, he showed pictures of him and Gal trying to avoid guards and then fighting them to escape the habitat.

"That is good. I will need time to consider your words. Unfortunately, we do not have nourishment for your kind. While we decide what to do with you, you should stay safe in this room we have used before with air-breathers. Be still, and we shall deliberate and let you know of our decision shortly."

The door swung shut, closing them in without any way to see what was going on beyond the walls that kept the water out and them imprisoned.

22
A Call To Arms

SKYLAR STARED at the closed door. It seemed to be a barrier of some sort that blocked his mental gifts from reaching out, almost the same way it kept the water from coming in. He'd been able to communicate with the Resmordian when the door was open so it wasn't just some kind of energy field imprisoning his thoughts. The fishman had been close, and that might've been part of it, but he hadn't been able to feel anyone else. There had to be an answer to what was blocking him from reaching Filzbalm and the others. He needed to work that out. If he could find them and let them know what was going on, he, Gal, and Teir might get rescued before the Resmordians decided what to do with them.

"They really don't like airbreathers," Gal said. "I've heard about that, but haven't actually had any dealing with the Resmordians before. It's all been myth and legends before now."

Skylar frowned and leaned against the door, crossing his arms. "Really? Del made it sound like you Tursiops had a decent relationship with them."

Gal shrugged. "Depends on who you talk to. I guess the Aduncuses do, since they make sure to follow all the rules set down in the treaty. They never over-fish the waters around their island, even though they do make most of their money shipping fish off world to the markets. But that's just the way they are. Some of the other families resent the limits the Resmordians put on us and the harvest we're allowed to take. Click's family is also big into restocking the fish they harvest. It's not overly hard to milk the fish for their sperm and eggs after they're taken. It can be very beneficial, but it's also time consuming, so a lot of families don't do it. That makes those families less popular with the Resmordians."

"Okay, that's good to know. Since we've got the Aduncus family on our side, hopefully that will work in our favor." But that wasn't helping them get out of the room and get word to the professor. "Gal, can you try to open the door?"

"Tried when I found out it was locked." Gal walked over and tapped on the door. "It's like it's sealed. There's nothing in the knob to unlock. There's no elocking mechanism either."

Skylar tried to think of any other way out. "But you didn't try to force it open with your telekinesis."

Gal leaned against the door. "The dampening field makes it hard to even think about doing that."

"I'd offer to help, but I don't think we need to burn down the room, even if the dampening field wasn't in place and I could access my powers," Teir said. "We'd use up all the oxygen fast, and that would be bad with us being under water."

Skylar nodded. "So, you can control fire. That's not one of the powers we're taught to use on Stars' End. I wonder if there's a record of it somewhere else? We'll have to get Del and Melody to do some research on that when we get out of here. Seems to be new powers popping up a lot lately."

"I know the people experimenting on us were excited by my gift when it came out." Teir sighed. "But they were really looking for movers. There was something about paying big money for movers."

"Movers are always in high demand," Gal said. "We're the most useful gift."

"Depends on how you look at it," Skylar countered. He'd been in several discussions at school about which gift was better. If Solaria was involved, it normally ended up being movers.

Gal held up his hand and shook his head. "Nope, not going there. You've got two gifts, and that crystal thing, which is like a gift unto itself. Not going to debate powers with you, Skylar. Besides, we've now got new powers to bring into the contest, and we don't know the full extent of how they work. Okay, Del can talk to AI's, but that doesn't really help much in the real world, does it? Just with that ship of yours. Teir here can set things on fire. Rather explosive, but how useful? We won't know until the professors from Stars' End can study him and catalogue him."

Shaking his head, Teir grumbled, "No. I'm done being studied and catalogued. I'm a person, not some strange science experiment."

Skylar put a hand on Teir's arm. "It won't be like that. We're going to need to work on getting your powers under control. It can take a lot of effort, particularly since you came into them late, like I did. Solaria and Del made things look easy while I was stumbling around like a blind mule trying to find my way through the forest."

Teir chuckled. "Remember that time we found that mule running into trees before it would go around them? It took us forever to round it up in the jungle and return it to its owner."

Skylar nodded. "Yeah. Luckily there weren't that many blind mule around Cordnisar, and the place was small enough for everyone to know everyone else."

The door swung open again. A Resmordian swam on the other side. It was impossible to tell if it was the same one or not.

"We have considered your words. With the domes in disarray, it is time for us to strike. We will take you with

us. If you are truly the Boarisks' enemies, then you will fight with us to drive them out of our waters." The image Skylar saw was a massive school of Resmordians rushing the domes—some of them were in protective bubbles and floated inside the dome. There was a distinct other-worldly feel to it—it wasn't as sharp and clear as the other images had been. It was what the Resmordian *wanted* to happen, not something that had already happened.

A soft blue glow, like the one that had engulfed them in the ocean outside the habitat, appeared in the center of the room. Seconds later, three envirosuits appeared.

"I guess we're going with them," Skylar said as he lifted the first suit. It looked a bit big for him, so he handed it to Gal.

"It's better than being in this room." Gal took the suit and began slipping it on over his loose-fitting clothes.

The second suit was too small, so Skylar handed it to Teir. Back on Hummassa they'd been closer to the same size. Since then he'd kept growing normally, but it was like Teir had stopped. Even if he didn't know everything Teir had been through, he knew enough to understand that his friend had scars, both mental and physical.

The final suit was closer to his size, although Skylar was sure it was going to be tighter than the suits he was used to. Even over the lightweight shirt and shorts he wore on Tursipia, it was a little encumbering. The helmet was different from the one he was used to as well. There was no way he'd be able to fit Filzbalm in there with him.

When he was suited up, Skylar glanced at Teir. He held his helmet in his hands and turned it over, staring at it.

"What's wrong?" Skylar asked.

"Not sure how this goes on," Teir replied. "I can tell you've put on esuits before, and we've done it in VR, but that's different. I don't know what I'm doing."

"Don't worry." Skylar took the helmet from him. "Solaria one time put hers on backwards when she was in a hurry." He slipped the helmet over Teir's head and fastened it to the collar of the suit. "It was funny at the time, but she was pissed off. A word of warning—an angry Pantherian can be very dangerous."

"Worse than a mad Pawleian? When they first came on the slave ship, several of them tried to take on the Boarisk guards. It wasn't pretty." Teir flexed his fingers like he was trying to get them settled into the gloves that were part of the suit, although they were permanently attached to the sleeves—another difference from the suits Skylar was used to that had separate gloves and boots.

"I've been around several Pantherians, both at school and away from it. They're very moody and very dangerous, unless they consider you family. Then you're safe." Skylar hoped he made it through the conflict with the Boarisks and got back to Solaria and her family, who were as much his family as Del and Melody were.

"I think we're ready," Gal said. "I wonder where they got these suits. They're standard deep-diving rigs that we use for oyster diving."

"You could ask him." Skylar pointed at the Resmordian beyond their threshold.

Gal shrugged. "You've been doing great communicating with him—I think I'll leave it up to you. Besides, you're mission leader."

Skylar rolled his eyes and walked over to the door, the strange flipper feet of the suit slapping against the floor with each step. *"I think we're ready."*

"And so are we." There was an image of a huge school of Resmordians, all carrying staves with their fins wrapped around the shafts.

After having seen the sticks open up some kind of portal, Skylar wondered if there was more they could do, or if the Resmordians were just going to use them to club the Boarisk and Orcans into submission.

Nearly a dozen Resmordians held their glowing staves and swam in a wide circle. The water around them luminesced a brilliant blue. Resmordians were already streaming through a portal that looked a lot like a stargate, but without the stars. They would reach the edge of the portal's event horizon and disappear, just like a starship going through a stargate.

As Teir, Gal, and Skylar exited the room, the field that had blocked Skylar from connecting to Filzbalm and the others lifted.

"Skylar!" Filzbalm shouted loud enough to make Skylar's eyes hurt.

"Filzbalm, where are you?" Skylar replied, not wanting to reprimand the Solar Drake, since he was happy to hear from him too.

"In the island. Solaria and I are trying to free the slaves, but the Boarisk are fighting back. They have us pinned down. Del, Leonada, and Click are trying to get to us, but they've encountered resistance. Professor Aduncus and the council troops are just now landing on the island."

Skylar swam in place once they were in the line of people…fish…beings…waiting for their turn through the portal. *"We'll be back in a few minutes. Let Solaria know. When we're through the Resmordian portal, I'll link us all up. The Resmordians are coming to fight."*

"I knew you were safe, but I couldn't find you," Filzbalm babbled. It wasn't something Skylar was used

to from the Solar Drake. It showed his level of worry about Skylar's disappearance.

Skylar and the others swam closer to the portal. It was almost their turn. *"I know. I couldn't feel you either. But we're both okay. You and Solaria stay safe. We'll be back real soon."*

Then it was time for Skylar to go through the portal. He swam forward. There was the same feeling as when he went through a stargate, then the ocean felt instantly different. He hadn't noticed it on the other side, but upon exiting the portal, he knew immediately that the ocean he was in was dead, totally incapable of supporting life.

Around him, the Resmordians swam forward, heading toward the domes at top speed, their glowing staves leaving streams of red light through the dark, dank water. He and Teir swam fast to keep up while Gal propelled himself along using his mover gift. Skylar hoped they all had what it took to stop the Boarisks and the Orcans.

23
The Battle Is Joined

SWIMMING MADE it hard for Skylar to concentrate on forming the gestalt with his friends, so Filzbalm took over for him. The crystal shard in his hand burned hot as Filzbalm reached through Skylar to it and then out to the others.

"I have sealed myself and am heading down under water," Astara said through her link with Del. She sounded distant, but still part of them.

"Leonada, Click, and I are heading to help Solaria," Del said, sounding stronger, as though he was right with them.

"We've got the slaves' barracks blocked at both doors," Solaria said. *"But they're working hard to get in to us. I can't tell if they're wanting to kill everyone, or just get through the room to get to the surface."*

"There are other routes to the surface," Leonada said. *"We saw them on Astara's scans. They must be trying to get to the prisoners. She's blocking their efforts to use the bracelets against their captives."*

"Then we have to stop them," Skylar said. *"Once we're into the habitat, we'll work on getting to the lift and to you from that side."*

"Skylar, you've got three coming in on you from behind," Solaria said.

Skylar looked back over his shoulder. The portal the Resmordians had opened was closed, but it looked like a group of Boarisk and Orcans was bearing down on them, riding single-person underwater transports that reminded him of some of the personal speeders people liked back on Hummassa.

"*Thanks.*" Skylar swam faster, not sure what he could do since he didn't have any weapons.

"*Stop and fight,*" Solaria shouted. "*They'll overtake you in just a moment and…oh, let me do it.*"

Her power surged through him. Two of the oncoming vehicles jerked violently, then careened into each other. Their riders tumbled off into the water.

"*Oh hey, good idea,*" Gal said seconds before more of the riders spun out of control.

The Resmordians turned and fired their staves, sending thick red bolts of energy at the guards, who were trying to swim back to their rides.

Boarisk and Orcans surged out of the hole in the dome. More of the Resmordians fired on them, but they fired back. The Resmordians swam hard and fast toward the dome, keeping up their barrage.

"*How many people are on the islands and in the habitats?*" Skylar asked as he swam to the left, trying to head around the defenders so he could get into the dome, hoping to pick up a weapon of some sort along the way.

"*This is a very large operation,*" Teir said. "*But a lot of them came and went on the ships that landed.*"

"*Okay, not totally helpful,*" Solaria said.

Suddenly, lights blazed in the dark water, making everything look like bright daylight and not a murky, deep ocean. Astara illuminated the battle scene, then began firing on the bad guys. She quickly laid waste to them.

Skylar thought about swimming to her but dismissed the idea. He needed to get into the habitat, get to the lift and up to help Solaria. "*Thanks, Astara. Stay down here and help the Resmordians, we're heading in to help get the slaves out.*"

"*Understood,*" was her only reply.

With the way cleared, Skylar headed toward the hole in the habitat, a little surprised that it hadn't been repaired since they were kidnapped by the Resmordians. A massive shadow passed between him and Astara's lights.

"There's a large ship trying to leave the dome," Astara said. *"Should I pursue it?"*

"Yes, please," Skylar replied. *"Wait until it's in the air and then bring it down. Might be able to rescue any prisoners they have that way."*

"That's logical," Astara agreed.

Skylar spotted one of the Resmordians floating belly up in the water, its staff sinking toward the ocean floor. He swam toward it, tapping into Solaria's power to draw the staff to him.

"Why are you collecting trophies again?" Del asked.

"I'm not. Unless I use someone's mover powers, I don't have any gifts that work on Boarisks. I need a weapon. If I can figure out how to use it." Skylar also wanted to figure out if the staves were part of the way the Resmordians made the portals or not. He figured that would take Del and Astara to figure out, but they would need a staff to do that. After seeing the Resmordians fire devastating bolts of power from them, he knew they also had offensive capabilities.

"Thanks," Solaria said. *"I'm using a lot of power to keep the door closed. These guys really want in here."*

Skylar and Teir cleared the edges of the hole in the dome. *"We're inside."* He glanced around and saw Gal grappling with a Boarisk who had been astride one of the vehicles. *"Gal, hurry up."*

Gal hit the Boarisk hard in the head, sending it tumbling end over end, then in a burst of telekinetic power shot across the remaining distance between himself and Skylar. *"Before we leave, I want to get one of those underwater bikes. They're great."*

"We'll get Astara to grab you one after the fighting's over," Skylar said as they started down the flooded corridor.

Above them something shook the dome, and a beam of light flashed across the broken, clear polycrete they'd just swam through.

"They got guns on the dome?" Fear shot through Skylar. He had no idea what that would do to the Resmordians who'd brought them back and were leading the assault. *"We've got to stop those guns."* He paused in his swimming as they reached heavy blast doors that hadn't been in the corridor when they'd been there earlier.

Skylar looked at Teir. *"Any idea where the controls for the gun might be?"*

Teir shook his head. *"They never let me explore. I don't know much."*

"How about how to get through the door?" Skylar didn't see any kind of panel to access it.

"I'm still in their computer systems," Astara said. *"I believe I can find the door controls. The weapons system is behind a firewall I haven't been able to break yet."*

"It's okay," Del said. *"There's a limit to how many calculations you can do at one time. Open the door and bring that ship down. Skylar will worry about the weapons. I think we're going to try to take down their power grid, see if that helps."*

"Ah, Del, don't do that just yet," Skylar said. *"Wait until we're out of the dome and back up to the island. Otherwise that will be a long climb, or a worse swim."* He wasn't even sure the lift had any way for them to climb up from the inside.

"You know Astara could just pick you up down there after this is all over," Del said. *"Wait a minute. We're*

encountering resistance on the surface. Click, block that beam."

"Working on it," Click said.

"Concentrate on your situation, we'll handle ours," Skylar said. Through their link he caught glimpses of Boarisk, Orcans, and others rushing out of the jungle firing blasters and projectile weapons at them.

"Skylar, we need to hurry," Solaria said. *"I don't know how long I can hold the doors. I'm drawing a little power off everyone, but I don't want to drain anyone and I've already gone through two stimpatches. We're all going to need some of our resources to get out of here."*

"I think I've got the door," Gal said. The blast door blocking their way opened and the water rushed forward to fill the dry corridor beyond.

"Close the door again!" Skylar shouted as the three of them were swept through the door and beyond.

"Trying to," Gal said, pulling power through the link to use it on the door mechanism hidden in the wall.

The door closed and the flow of water stopped.

Gal and Teir found their feet as Skylar tried to get the strange flipper-like ends of his envirosuit sorted out so he could stand. He was much more comfortable with the standard suits that didn't have specialty shoes attacked.

"Now where?" Gal asked.

"We need to stop the weapon and then get to Solaria." Skylar said, pulling off his helmet. He really wanted to get rid of the whole suit, but wasn't sure what he would do if he did that and the dome cracked more. Swimming in the deep water without it wouldn't be much fun.

"You guys okay?" Filzbalm asked. *"You got quiet."*

"Yeah, we're fine. We're out of the water and able to talk verbally again." The link with everyone was still strong. Not having to concentrate on swimming while

speaking was going to make it easier to coordinate the team.

"I know the main control system isn't in this wing," Teir said. "This is the lab and training wing."

"So back toward the lift then, maybe it's over there," Skylar said, hoping they would be able to find the place quickly.

"Astara's working on getting a map for us," Del said. *"She's got the ship that's trying to flee in her sights, but it's armed and giving her fits."*

"Thanks, Del. We know where some computers are. Maybe we can find it that way." Skylar glanced around. The water ended at the door where he and Gal had found the lab. If they could get back into the computers, they could find out where the control room was.

"Good. These guys up here are setting up a perimeter around their compound. They're trying to keep us out."

Solaria chuckled. *"Then it's a good thing some of us are already behind their lines. As soon as we can, we'll be with you, Del."*

"Thanks." There was a flash as something near Del exploded. A pull of power ran through their group mind as Click blocked a shot. *"Need to concentrate here."*

Conversation dropped off.

"In here," Skylar ran into the room they'd been in before. The lights were on, and the room beyond the observation room was larger than Skylar had figured. There were twenty or so beds with lots of equipment that he was unfamiliar with.

"Let's do this." Gal rushed over to the computer he'd been at previously. It was still booted and he started going through files and data.

"I'll watch the hall," Teir said, with a definite tremble in his voice. Fear rolled off him before he turned back to the doorway.

Skylar left Gal working to find their path to the control room and went to Teir. "This is where they experimented on you, isn't it?"

Teir hugged himself. "Yeah."

"I'm sorry. I didn't know. This is the closest computer." Skylar wished he could prevent his friend from feeling more pain, even if was just the memory of pain.

"It's okay. I understand." Teir didn't sound like it was okay. "We're doing what we can to shut them down. That's the important thing. I'll get through this, then I never want to see another Boarisk."

"What if we can make them all pay for what they've done?" Skylar was torn between helping people and bringing the Boarisk to justice for what they were up to. It wasn't just about what they'd destroyed on Hummassa. It went beyond just getting vengeance for his mother. They were destroying entire ecosystems, corrupting people without their permission, creating a blight on the universe. He wanted to make sure they were stopped, once and for all.

"As long as my mother is safe from them, I'd do anything to balance the scales over what they've done to everyone weaker than they are." For a moment, flames danced across Teir's hands. "Ironically, they've given me the power to make them pay."

Skylar squeezed Teir's shoulder. "The fire for vengeance they instilled in me has served me well too." He felt like he was finding new ground with his old friend. "We must stop them and help the weak. We are stronger because of them."

"You're both sounding like Pantherians down there," Solaria said. *"I think we've got the room secured for the moment. They suddenly stopped pounding on the door up here."*

"They might be regrouping to secure the island, thinking you're not a threat right now," Teir said. *"They may have also sealed that section off so you can't get out. That's one of the tactics they taught us in training."*

"That might not be a good thing," Skylar said. *"Filzbalm, make sure that the air doesn't get cut to there. I wouldn't put it past them to just decide to kill everyone and try to escape. If Astara wasn't blocking their use of the bracelets they'd probably just kill the prisoners."*

"It's flowing right now," Filzbalm replied.

"I've got the control center," Gal announced. "But it's going to be a bit of a challenge to get there. It's two domes over, and it looks like there's a ton of guards gathering in the corridors between here and there."

"That could definitely be a problem," Skylar agreed.

"Then do the unexpected," Solaria said. *"Prey always expects predators to act in a particular way. When you do the unexpected you can take them by surprise."*

Skylar had no clue what she was getting at. *"What do you suggest?"*

"Swim there." She sounded a bit smug. *"You still have your envirosuits don't you?"*

"The Resmordians are still fighting out there, but it might be easier than taking the corridors," Skylar agreed, bouncing the Resmordian staff in his hand. *"Thanks."*

"We're stronger together than individually."

"Gal, can you get the blast door open again?" Skylar started back toward the hall.

"Sure. It might take things a couple of minutes to equalize once we let water into this section." Gal started putting his helmet back on. "I'm presuming we want to flood this place if we head back out."

It would cause more confusion and damage in the habitat. Skylar nodded. "Sure. Let's do that. When we get outside again, we should stick close to the domes, try to avoid the battle out there if we can. The sooner we're in the other dome, the sooner we can shut down that gun and get moving." As he said that, he wondered how they were going to make it to the lift that would take them back to Solaria and the slave barracks. If the corridors were crowded with guards it might be harder than they wanted to deal with.

But if they had to deal with it, they would. He just wished his own powers would work against Boarisk. He didn't want to have to pull too much from the others.

Skylar and Teir found handholds on a rail that ran along the clear wall near the door before Gal opened it again. Even though Skylar felt ready when the torrent of water came rushing over him, he was still nearly ripped from his hold. For several minutes the freed ocean fought to fill the opening in the habitat. Somewhere in the distance claxons rang and people shouted. Skylar didn't care. It was only a matter of time before the ocean wiped the habitat out of existence—they were just doing their part to speed the process.

The water stopped pushing against them as it filled the corridor and all the rooms that were open to it. As the water pressure eased up, Skylar stared swimming.

"Alright, we're good to go down here," Skylar said, following Gal who shot ahead of them using his mover powers to get down the corridor quickly and to the opening into the ocean.

The battle outside the dome was still in full fury. The Resmordians had found their rhythm and were evading the shots from the weapon on the central dome all while engaging the Boarisk and Orcans, who were attempting to stop them. A good number of bodies from both sides littered the waters.

The memory of the people killed on Pantheria flashed in Skylar's mind, along with the loss of the cows on Stars' End. He'd been witness to so much death since the night the Boarisk attacked Hummassa. He wondered if it was ever going to end, or if his life was always going to be filled with death.

24
Stopping The Gun

"SKYLAR!" GAL'S shout drew Skylar's attention away from the battle.

Gal floated next to one of the Boarisk vehicles. There were several more near him. *"Let's use these. They're just floating here. If I test drive it, I'll know for sure if I want one."*

"Sure. It'll be faster than swimming." Anything that sped them up was welcome at this point. Skylar and Teir swam over to him.

Skylar settled into the seat, and grabbed the handlebars that reminded him a bit of the bike he'd had back in his childhood. But his bike didn't come with an O'Byrne Corp logo in the middle of the handlebars. He never thought about it before, but it made him wonder if there was any kind of transport that O'Byrne Corp didn't make. *"Any idea how they work?"*

A jet of bubbles shot out of the back of Gal's vehicle and it moved forward a bit. *"Okay. Twist the handle forward to get it to go. Just like a speeder bike."*

Teir moved before Skylar did. *"And backward to stop?"*

"Yeah," Gal said, and went racing past Teir.

Skylar did as Gal said. The force of the bike shooting forward pushed him back into the seat hard. He was thankful for his envirosuit and its helmet. If he hadn't had them, he wasn't sure he'd have been able to keep himself from taking a huge drink of the ocean as the bike propelled them across the top of the damaged dome.

Teir raced alongside him.

"*Okay you guys, don't wreck those,*" Solaria said. "*They look like way too much fun. We're going to have to use them when this is all over.*"

"*They are fun,*" Gal agreed. "*I'm keeping one.*"

As they topped the dome and started across toward the next one, the one with the gun mounted on its peak, Skylar wasn't sure if he wanted to keep one of the craft or not. He was having trouble maintaining a grip on the Resmordian staff and making the vehicle go the direction he wanted it to.

"*I'm surprised they aren't shooting at us,*" Teir said as they passed the gun.

"*Maybe since we're on the bikes,*" Gal said, "*they don't realize we aren't them.*"

Skylar slowed his craft. "*Wait a minute. We're driving past the gun, to go turn it off…that's stupid. Let's break it from out here.*"

Gal and Teir turned and came back to him.

"*That's a great idea.*" Gal stopped his waterbike, stood up on the seat and stared at the gun. Static danced across the surface of the weapon. Parts began to fly off of it. Then it exploded.

The concussion wave hit them hard, sending them and their watercraft tumbling backwards. Skylar bounced off the top of the dome and curled into a ball, frantically holding onto the staff as his bike rolled over the top of him. He lost all sense of direction as he somersaulted through the water.

"*Skylar!*" Filzbalm's shout hurt.

"*Filzbalm, use some restraint,*" Solaria scolded. "*That was too loud. We're all going to have a headache for hours.*"

"*I think I'm okay,*" Skylar said as he slowed. "*Gal took out the gun.*" He slowly straightened out and looked around for Gal and Teir.

They weren't swimming. They were both floating flat in the water. *"Gal? Teir? You two okay?"* Skylar swam toward Teir who was closest to him.

Neither one of them responded.

Skylar swam faster.

"I can reach Teir's mind," Filzbalm said. *"I think he's okay, just knocked out by the concussive wave."*

"What about Gal?" Skylar reached Teir just as he opened his eyes.

"I can't reach him," Filzbalm said.

"Teir, anything broken?" Skylar asked, then realized if his friend had been injured they'd all feel it through the link. All he felt from Gal was emptiness. There was a spot where he should've been, but he wasn't there.

"I still can't reach Gal," Filzbalm said.

"I'll be fine," Teir said. *"Go see about Gal."*

Gal had floated a short distance away in the time it had taken Skylar to reach Teir. Skylar had to swim harder to get to him. He grabbed Gal's arm and tried to feel something from him, but there was nothing. Skylar's heart raced as he tried to decide what to do.

"He's gone, Skylar," Del said. *"There's nothing from him. No thoughts, no emotions, no anything. If Grandfather was here he could check from the least little bit of brain activity, but he's not here. He was too close to the explosion. He may have been trying to shield the three of you from the blast. Odds are he saved you and Teir."*

Skylar stared at the wreckage of the gun. Something deep inside him went ice cold. *"It was my idea. If we'd stuck to the plan and gone inside to cut the power he'd still be alive."*

"You don't know that," Del and Teir said at the same time. The words echoed oddly in their group mind.

"Look, Gal was a big boy," Click spoke up for the first time in a while. Sadness tinged his mental voice, reminding Skylar he'd been the one to ask Gal to come with them. *"He would've known there was a chance of that thing blowing up when he went to destroy it. He was your mover. He could've told you no, or told you to use that staff of yours, but he didn't. He took the chance. The gun's gone. We'll sing of his courage later. Now we have a battle to win. Get inside and help Solaria."*

"We're taking fire here," Del said. *"Take Teir and get inside to help Solaria and Filzbalm."*

"We don't mourn our warriors until the battle is done," Leonada said. *"And now we need to fight."*

From the images the three of them were projecting, they had people closing in on their position, and it was all they could do to keep themselves safe.

"I've got the ship down," Astara cheered with more emotion than an AI should have.

"Good. At least something is going right." Skylar turned and looked at Teir. *"What do you think we should do?"* He was worried about making a decision and getting them both killed. He'd already caused enough death.

Teir was turning his waterbike over to get back on it. *"If Gal was right and the halls are crawling with guards, then maybe we need to head up to the island and go in that way. At least if I'm in air and not water, I can use my powers to help out."*

"That's actually a good idea," Del threw in. *"All the islands have airlocks in the lower parts. They're maintenance hatches. You might be able to bypass trouble that way."*

With the Resmordians and the bad guys fighting around the domes, it made sense. Skylar swam over to his watercraft and followed Teir's example. It made him feel a little better following someone else's lead for a while.

He didn't like the emotion of loss, the knowledge that if he hadn't changed the plan, Gal would still be with them and not floating away to be lost in the ocean depths.

His bike started easily and he aimed it up toward the surface. Skylar couldn't help but glance toward the main battlefield. So many Resmordians floated dead among the Boarisk and the Orcans. It made Skylar wonder how long they were going to fight before they created their portal and fled to safer waters. He wasn't going to be able to do that until he knew that all his remaining friends were safe.

25
To The Rescue

AS THEY followed the lift tubes up, Skylar hoped their envirosuits would be able to adjust to the change in water pressure and keep them from getting sick by going up too fast. He'd heard stories on documentaries of divers on Hummassa who liked to dive with as little equipment as possible as a challenge. Sometimes they got sick from the pressure change. Just swimming around the domes had been one thing—going up was something different, with more risks.

"If those are suits you got from the Resmordians you should be fine," Del said. *"They're made by Tursiops for deep diving."*

"We're in this mind link too deep," Skylar said. *"I was just worrying about that, I didn't actually ask you the question."*

"This is the longest we've been linked like this," Del said. *"That might have something to do with it. But then I'm not hearing Click or Teir the way I am you and Solaria."*

"I was wondering about that too," Solaria chimed in. *"This time it's almost as deep as your bond with Filzbalm, or at least I guess that's what your bond is like."*

"It is," Filzbalm said.

"We need to ask Grandfather about this," Del said. *"But right now, we need to concentrate on our situations. I'm going to divert energy to Click. He, and Leonada, are keeping us alive up here. I'm useless."*

"You're not useless," Astara piped in. *"You've got me. And I'll be there in minutes to shoot them for you. I've got the ship locked in my tractor beam and have shut down their computers."*

"I'm glad one of our teams is working right," Skylar said. He glanced over his shoulder. They were so far up in the dark waters he couldn't see the fight happening below him. Even the lights of the domes were little more than liquid stars flickering in the dark water.

For several minutes, silence closed in on Skylar. If he concentrated on one person, he could sense what was going on around them. Solaria and Filzbalm were also having a pause in their excitement. Solaria had secured one of the doors into the barracks, and the prisoners had blocked the other one with cots and chairs. Filzbalm rested on Solaria's shoulder as she talked to Taglia, assuring her Teir was okay and coming toward them quickly. Del and the others were behind a boulder on a hill overlooking the compound. They hadn't been completely surrounded by the island defenders, but they were getting closer by the second.

Worrying about his friends wasn't going to help. Professor Aduncus always told Skylar to try to keep his emotions under control in order to keep his focus.

An energy blast barely missed Skylar, churning the water as it passed him. It missed Teir too.

Skylar glanced over his shoulder. Two Boarisk on watercraft were following close behind. *"Any ideas?"* Skylar asked. He really didn't want to get shot in the back if they continued up.

Teir swung his bike around and headed back toward them. *"I don't have my control bracelets on anymore. They can't stop me from hurting them."*

Following his example, Skylar angled toward the Boarisk Teir wasn't heading toward. Through the Boarisk's faceplate, the look of surprise was obvious as

Skylar used the Resmordian staff like a lance. The Boarisk tried to twist out of the way and stay on his cycle, but the staff caught him in the side of the head, knocking him off his vehicle and sending it spinning into the lift tube. There was a crash and air rushed out of the tube as water filled it. With the air bubbling around them, Skylar swung the staff hard, hoping it would handle the abuse of hitting a Boarisk.

The bubbles confused him, but he managed to strike a hard blow against the Boarisk's helmet. Swinging the staff in water was a lot harder that using it the same way in air would've been, and the water seemed to soften the blow.

There were several small buttons on the staff. His gloves were just thin enough to let him find where they were positioned, aligned with a small strap that was the perfect size for a hand or a fin. Although he had no clue what effect it would have, he started tapping them, hoping one of them would do something. The Resmordians had been firing them like blasters.

The Boarisk slammed into him as he was fumbling with the staff and got its thick arms around his waist. Its helmet hurt his ribs where it impacted him. Skylar kicked as hard as he could, but it didn't seem to do any good. His defenses didn't help him dislodge the Boarisk. He hit it again several times with the staff as he continued tapping buttons. Something he did made the staff hum, and pulled psychic power out of him.

A glowing red beam of force erupted from the staff. It caught the Boarisk right in the helmet. The clear plexy shattered and Skylar's attacker spun backward away from him, tumbling end over end through the water.

"Teir." Skylar glanced around.

"Over here." Teir floated several feet behind Skylar. His hands glowed orange as he punched his opponent through its shattered faceplate. He let the

Boarisk go and swam back to where his watercraft floated, waiting for him to continue his journey up the outside of the lift tube.

"You okay?" Skylar asked as he swam back to his own vehicle.

"I think so. I don't think they were prepared for us to be anything other than helpless." There was a bitterness in Teir's tone that Skylar understood.

"They aren't making this easy, are they?" Del said. *"Although Astara's guns just came in real handy. I'm glad we kept those as part of her design."*

"It always pays to be properly armed," Solaria added.

Skylar got on his watercraft and continued up toward the bottom of the island, wishing he could keep his mind open for more unexpected attacks, but unless they were Orcans, it wouldn't do him any good. The Boarisk's natural immunity to psychic attacks irritated him more and more every day.

ONCE THEY reached the bottom of the island, which was tapered like the keel of a boat, it took Skylar and Teir some time to actually locate an airlock. Even with Astara trying to get them there, they had trouble finding their way along the barnacle-encrusted underside to their destination. The barnacles formed a thick covering, and once they located the airlock they struggled to get it open.

As the water automatically drained away once they cycled the inner airlock hatch, Skylar wondered if it would be better to lose the envirosuit, or keep it on. They hadn't encountered any problems with water when he'd been in the underbelly of the island before, and the flippers made it hard to move quietly when he was out of water.

"Whatever you do, hurry," Solaria called out when the water was about to his knees. *"They're trying to get through again. A little more forcefully this time. You know, I could really use a stimpatch. The last one faded a little while ago."*

"No, you're fine just drawing power from the rest of us." Skylar pushed his fears that Solaria was wanting stimpatches too often out of his head. He had to focus on getting out of the airlock and up to them.

"We'll start down from the top," Del said. *"If we can clear the way from here, you can get out."*

"Sounds good." Solaria growled at something near her but didn't provide a mental picture so Skylar wasn't sure what it was. *"Also, if you haven't already, have Astara jam their coms again. That might add to their confusion and buy us more time."*

"On it," Astara replied.

Skylar tapped at the airlock's inner door, wishing the water would finish draining so the door would open.

"I say leave the suits," Teir said, already pulling off his helmet. "We'll move faster and quieter without them. I guess it's too much to ask fishmen to have clothing without fins."

"Probably." Skylar turned from the inner door control panel, leaned the staff against the wall and followed Teir's example. His helmet made a splash in the ankle-high water when he dropped it. The envirosuit was harder to remove when it was wet. He yanked at it several times to get it off his shoulders after he opened the front and when he finally pulled it down to his feet, the flippers seemed stuck to the point that Skylar stumbled backward until he was at the wall and could balance better.

By the time he flung the suit to the floor, the water was gone, drained away to the ocean outside and leaving only a few puddles here and there. Teir had managed to

get his suit off faster and was tapping on the control
panel to open the door.

"I definitely like my suit back on Astara better,"
Skylar mumbled as he flattened out his shirt and shorts.
"It fits me."

"I never thought either one of us would end up with
our own envirosuit," Teir said as he got the door open.
"At least one of us is living out the adventures we always
dreamed about as we were gaming."

Skylar shrugged. "I guess so. For the most part,
most of my time has been in class—sure, they're
different classes than what we had on Hummassa, but I'm
still a student." Even as he said it, he realized he was a lot
more than just a student. He'd rescued people, explored
strange worlds he'd only heard about in books, even been
part of a space battle. Although he'd not sought out any
of his adventures before the one he was on, he seemed to
stumble into them a lot.

"It still sounded like fun when you were telling me
about it back in our little room-cell under the ocean."
Teir sounded sad as he started walking down the hallway.

"Let's see what the next few hours bring, and see
what your mother says when we rescue her. Maybe you
can stay and study with us on Aduncus Island. Astara
should have an extra berth or two. I'm sure Del wouldn't
mind you joining our crew."

Teir nodded. "Let's rescue Mom and see what she
has to say. But we never know, Stars' End might not
want someone like me."

"Like you?" Skylar didn't think there were any
kinds of psychics Stars' End would turn away.

"Gene-augmented."

"Don't be silly," Skylar said as they rounded a
corner, then clamped his mouth shut.

Three guards, two Boarisks and an Orcan were
walking toward them, guns drawn.

"Hey, stop!" one of the Boarisk shouted.

"No, you stop." Teir squinted and pointed at them. Power rolled off him. Seconds later, the two Boarisks burst into flames.

"No, you don't." The Orcan stared at them. "I can shut you down."

Skylar stepped in front of Teir and got a mental shield up around the two of them. If they weren't linked in the gestalt with the others, he wasn't sure if he'd have been able to do that. He protected them from the Orcan's assault, then shoved it back at him.

The Boarisks were screaming, rolling around on the floor trying desperately to put the flames out as the Orcan struggled to block Skylar's return of his attack.

"You need to sleep." Skylar projected the thought into the Orcan's mind as hard as he could. The Orcan put his hands on the side of his smooth black and white head, then collapsed to the floor.

The Boarisks' screams stopped as they ceased moving. Their charred corpses lay on the floor and the smell of fried bacon filled the corridor.

Teir stared at the Boarisks he'd killed. "I've never pushed it that far before."

Patting Teir's shoulder, Skylar still remember the knot in his stomach the first time something had died at his hands. He wished he could've spared Teir the experience, but they were at war, and he understood that people died in war. He glanced at the Orcan laying on the floor near the burned bodies. Depending on what happened to the island and when, he might die without ever waking up. At least it would be gentler than the Boarisks being burned alive. "We all understand. No matter how much we want them to suffer, it's hard to kill."

"Speak for yourself, Skylar," Solaria piped in. *"You did good, Teir. Your powers are impressive. Now get up*

here. They're trying to hack through the door. If the door goes, I don't know how long my telekinetic shield can hold them out."

"They are almost to you," Astara added. *"Two more turns. Professor Aduncus is approaching the island. The shields here have caused them difficulty in getting a lock on our location. I am having to assist."*

"We're on the way." Skylar glanced at Teir. "Come on. We've got to keep moving."

With a heavy sigh and pursed lips, Teir nodded. "Yeah we do."

Skylar hoped Solaria and Filzbalm would be able to hold off the Boarisk for a little longer. He knew the prisoners didn't have any weapons.If the Boarisk got in and defeated Solaria and Filzbalm, they would most likely kill the slaves in an effort to hide the evidence of their illegal operation. He didn't want to let that happen, for several reasons.

26
Reunion

THEY CAME around the last turn, a corridor Skylar had walked with Gal and Taglia earlier. A squad of Boarisks and Orcans stood looking like they were waiting for the large Boarisk with the axe to get through the door.

"That looks like them," Skylar said as they eased back around the corner.

"So what do we do?" Teir asked. He peered around the corner again. *"There's a lot of them. More than I think I can burn up quickly."*

"That was a bit nasty," Skylar said, wondering how long it was going to be before he could eat bacon again without flashing back on the dead Boarisks.

"We're almost to the door on the other side," Del announced. *"Not hitting a ton of resistance since Astara took out the ones topside."*

"We've got them on both doors," Solaria said. *"Honestly, I could really use a stimpatch here."*

"We're almost there," Skylar said. He was well aware of how much power she was drawing through their gestalt—their joint mental reservoir was quickly draining between her pulling energy and the occasional use of the others.

"Skylar, Del, where are you all?" Professor Aduncus asked. *"We have arrived on the island. Astara had to lead us here, as we couldn't penetrate their shield."*

"We're about to rescue Solaria and the prisoners," Del said. *"Can you join our link and lend us power? We're almost empty."*

"I'm sending government troops in your direction," the professor said. *"While you wait for them, take what you need from me."*

Skylar wanted to cheer, but didn't want to make any extra noise that might alert the guards that they were around the corner. He glanced at the staff. He knew which button to hit to get a power beam to come out, but he hadn't played around with it, and didn't know exactly what it was capable of.

"Okay, what if you hit a couple of them with your fire, and I blast them with the staff?" It wasn't the greatest plan in the galaxy, but it was the best he could come up with. From what he'd seen, all the guards at the door were Boarisks, so he couldn't do anything against them.

"Not the best, but I think it's all we got." Teir stared at Skylar for a minute. "You guys have been working with this group mind thing for a while, haven't you?"

"Yeah." Skylar really didn't think it was the best time for them to be discussing a very complex psychic talent. "What about it?"

"I can hear the others in my head. I can see what they're witnessing right now." He smiled softly. "It's been nice seeing my mother again. I haven't been with her in months. But how do I draw power from it? I presume I can tap into everyone else's power, like the professor who's just come."

Skylar nodded. He didn't want to think about how nice it would be to see his own mother. He needed to keep his focus. They were almost through with their part of the fight, but everything could be lost if he got distracted. "Yeah, you should be able to draw power from the gestalt like the rest of us can. Wait. If I can use one of the movers' gifts then I should be able to create a battering ram of telekinetic power, knocking them down. I like it."

"But I might be able to get a wide fire attack in there as well. More power means more that I can do, right?"

"Yeah. I like this." Skylar knew how to draw from just one member of their link. He didn't want to draw power from Solaria when she was trying to keep the door closed from her side. Click's mover powers were nearly as strong as Solaria's though. Augmented with the group power, he could make it work.

"We're engaging the guards on this side," Del called out.

"We've got a plan for over here," Skylar replied, hoping he wasn't going to disrupt things too much by tapping into Click's power. He didn't want to be responsible for someone else's death.

"Teir. I'm going to knock them down, you use your fire to confuse them, then I'm going to try picking them off one at a time with the staff." Skylar reached for Click, felt his mover gift and tapped into it so he could use the power. Click wasn't as used to working with all of them, not like Solaria, Del and Filzbalm were, but the gentle pulse of the crystal in Skylar's hand smoothed things over and as Skylar stepped around the corner again, he unleashed a blast of telekinetic force that spread out across the width of the corridor and slammed the guards hard against the wall before they even knew he was behind them. When he stopped the attack, they crumpled to the wall.

It didn't seem honorable to attack from behind but they were Boarisk, who raided planets in the dark of night when people weren't prepared and slaughtered anyone they didn't think was suitable for slavery. They didn't deserve his thoughts of honor.

Teir's power danced across Skylar's skin a second before a wall of flame appeared between them and the guards who were trying to get back to their feet. He was pulling through the gestalt link, but with Professor

Aduncus quietly providing extra power, they were able to handle it.

"I'm making it as hot as I can," Teir said. "I've never felt this strong."

"Being part of a mental link can help you grow," Solaria said. *"My powers are increasing like crazy since Skylar figured out how to do this. Wow, I can feel the heat through the door."*

"Be careful, young Mr. Puddle," Professor Aduncus added. *"I can tell your psychic channels are only roughly formed. Too much energy could burn you out."*

"I can regulate him if you want, Professor," Filzbalm said. *"I formed this current link."*

"We can monitor the situation, Filzbalm." Professor Aduncus went quiet as Skylar lifted the staff.

Having the Professor there in thought helped bolster Skylar's spirits. They were almost done. They could do this. They could save the prisoners and get everyone off the island while the authorities dealt with the rest of the Boarisks and Orcans.

One of the Boarisk staggered to his feet, looking terrified. Before it had a chance to do anything to them, Skylar pointed the staff and fired. The beam of power pulled at Skylar's personal energy reserves as the orange ray of force lanced out of it and hit the Boarisk Skylar had been aiming at. There was a squeal from the Boarisk and it hit the wall behind it and slid down, leaving a trail of blood from the hole in its torso.

Skylar tried to block out the scene and fired the staff again like they'd planned. After several shots, over half of the Boarisk were down.

"Watch where you're firing that thing," Solaria said. *"We're coming out."*

The remains of the door the Boarisk had been trying to get through exploded out into the corridor, hitting several of the guards as it went. Skylar picked off a couple more, then Solaria and Filzbalm were in the passageway. Even through the flames of Teir's firewall, the energy glow around Solaria's hand, as she punched the nearest guard, was visible to Skylar.

He fired the staff at the same one Filzbalm went after. The Boarisk went down easily, then Teir finished them off with a wave of fire that raced across the corridor floor and picked up size and heat as it crossed the firewall before burning the remaining Boarisk.

As the flames consumed the guards, the corridor reeked of charred flesh. Skylar fought back the urge to gag. Then the flames vanished.

Solaria stood a couple of feet from the doorway with her hands on her hips and a predatory look in her slitted eyes. "At least I got to punch one of them." She shook her head. "Okay, it stinks out here."

Filzbalm landed on Skylar's shoulder and wrapped his tail against Skylar's neck. *"We were separated. I couldn't find you. Don't do that again."*

Skylar laughed and rubbed the Solar's Drake's head, paying close attention to his horns. "I'll do my best. The Resmordians had us in a psi-blocked room deep underwater. I'll try to stay out of those in the future."

"See that you do."

There was a rush of feet and a female squeal. Skylar glanced up from Filzbalm just in time to see Teir and his mother come together in the middle of the hall.

Taglia hugged him tightly as she sobbed. "You're okay. I never thought I'd see you again."

"I'm okay, Mom." Teir hugged her back, burying his face in her hair.

Skylar wanted to give them a little space. He didn't want to interfere with their reunion. They deserved to be happy, even in the midst of charred Boarisk.

"Do we need to go hit the ones on the other side of the barracks?" Skylar asked.

"I think we've got them," Del replied. *"We're lucky Boarisk aren't immune to movers the way they are readers and feelers."*

"Totally different power base," Professor Aduncus said. *"The planetary forces will be to your location momentarily. You should all start to make your way to the surface and to Astara. From what I'm hearing on com channels the way should be clear."*

"Good." Skylar walked through the remains of the door and into the slave barracks. The former prisoners stood there staring that him as if they were waiting for him to do something. He took a couple of steps into the room and realized that some of them still had their control bracelets on, while others didn't.

He turned and looked at Solaria who was leaning against the door looking tired. "Have you been working on getting their bracelets off?"

She nodded. "Yeah. The tricky part was blocking the incoming signal on the second one after the first one came off. Luckily, Astara was helping. They also tend to explode once they're removed." She pointed over to several of the beds that had large holes in them. "Luckily nobody got hurt when they went off. Limited area of effect on those things."

"It would probably be a bad thing to arm your workforce with powerful explosives if you can help it," Skylar said, wondering if any of the prisoners ever committed suicide by rushing the guards while yanking their bracelets off.

Taglia screamed in the hallway.

Skylar turned so fast that Filzbalm had to dig into his shirt and through the leather pad there for him to keep from falling off. Rushing next to Solaria, Skylar made it a few steps into the hallway before he spotted the huge Boarisk that was holding Teir up by his neck. The thing was the biggest Boarisk Skylar had ever seen, over seven feet tall and half as broad, looking like it was all muscle. Taglia lay crumbled on the floor.

"Stop, children," the Boarisk said. "You and those stupid fish warriors have cost me much today, but I am keeping this one. He is the pride of our work here. The strongest we have made. You cannot have him."

Teir kicked at the Boarisk, but for some reason wasn't using his powers.

A thick black collar was on Teir's neck.

"That must be a dampening collar," Solaria said.

"Makes sense." Skylar knew they had to come up with something quickly. If they attacked the Boarisk, he could snap Teir's neck before they could take him down.

"Put down that staff, boy. I have seen what it can do. Who would've expected fish to make weapons?"

Kneeling, Skylar complied as he reached for Teir's mind. He was still part of the gestalt. The collar wasn't blocking him from that. *"Teir. Can you burn the collar out like you did the control bracelets?"*

"I think so, but I don't want to hurt Mom. I don't even know if she's okay. He hit her really hard." Fear tainted his words.

"She's only unconscious," Professor Aduncus said. *"I think she's got a concussion."*

"Then we need to get her out of here and to Astara's med bay," Skylar said. *"Okay. Teir take out the collar, I'm taking out the Boarisk."*

Skylar slowly rose from putting the staff down and held his hand up trying to look like he was surrendering as he tapped into Teir's power. He stared at the Boarisk. "Now what?" He molded the flaming energy into a needle of force and drove it into the Boarisk's eye before he could answer.

Teir burst into flames. Every bit of his body was covered in fire.

The Boarisk dropped him and grabbed his face, pawing ineffectively with his hoof-like fingers to put out the flames that shot out of his eye and engulfed his snout.

As he turned to run, Teir grabbed him, still flaming.

The Boarisk screamed as the flames consumed him. Teir continued holding on to him, drawing power through their gestalt, making the fire hotter and hotter as his tormentor died.

"Teir, stop, you're pulling too much!" Professor Aduncus yelled through all their minds.

"I'm cutting him off," Filzbalm said.

Then Teir's flames died. Teir let go of the Boarisk's charred remains and staggered several steps before catching himself on the wall. Somehow his clothes and skin weren't damaged from the fire he'd used. He shook as he stood there, one hand on the wall supporting him.

Del and Leonada ran into the corridor. "Okay. We're here," Del announced.

"We need to get Taglia out of here," Skylar said. "I'll get Teir if you guys can get his mother."

"I've got her." Solaria picked Taglia up, looking like she was trying her best to be as gentle as possible.

Skylar touched Teir's shoulder. "We've got your mother, come on. We need to get out of here."

Teir paused and stared at the cooked corpse he'd recently had hold of. "It's over, isn't it?"

"I hope so," Skylar replied. "I really hope so."

He helped Teir through the barracks where Click was getting the last of the control bracelets off the prisoners, so they could go up the ladder to the storage building Skylar had discovered. With Taglia still unconscious, it took a bit of work between Solaria and Leonada to get her up without jostling her too much, but they did it. They were both too tired to try using their powers to lift her up. All of them were drained.

Skylar had never been so happy to get out into the fresh air of a planet before. Even being trapped underground in Pantheria hadn't been as bad as underwater and in the habitats. A group of Tursiops in military gear met them before they made it more than a couple of steps. Del stepped up and talked with them, while directing Skylar and the others to keep heading to the beach where they always parked Astara.

Not feeling up to arguing, Skylar took the lead and hurried them as fast as they could. He was ready to be off the island, but other than Gal, there hadn't been major injuries on their part.

Gal hadn't purposely sacrificed himself like Solaria's Aunt Blizza had. He'd just been following Skylar's lead. Skylar didn't like the thought that he'd gotten Gal killed. It wasn't right, and he wanted to find a way to make amends.

27
Taking Responsibility

IT HAD been three days since they rescued Teir and the others. There had been several celebrations on Aduncus Island. Skylar and his friends had been the honored guests at each one of them, but Skylar was getting tired of it. He didn't feel like a hero. He'd done what he felt was right, but people had died. That didn't make him a hero. Heroes were supposed to be always right and never let anyone die. He hadn't done that. Gal wasn't coming home. More than a few of the Resmordians weren't coming home. Sure, the Boarisks' and Orcans' mining and gene-manipulation projects were foiled, but there had been a lot of losses.

Skylar lay in his bunk on Astara and stared at the ceiling. There were always costs. He understood that, but was just getting tired of having major ramifications to everything he did. It didn't seem fair.

Solar Drakes and researchers had died while he was trying to get Filzbalm back to his people. Sure, that hadn't been directly his fault, and honestly he and the others saved lives with their intervention, but people still died. The final death toll was still being tallied on Pantheria, and although he knew a few of them, the one that really hit him was Blizza, who'd sacrificed herself to stop Freyandor, the ancient, final member of the original inhabitants of Pantheria. He only hoped that when it came time for him to make a similar choice, he could find the courage to do what Blizza did to save her people and planet.

But Gal's death had been directly due to Skylar's decisions and actions. That wasn't fair. He'd made a mistake, and someone had paid the ultimate price for it.

A knock came from Skylar's cabin door.

In what had become a reflex, Skylar reached out his mind and checked to see who it was as he sat up.

Teir.

"Come in," Skylar called.

As the door opened, Filzbalm stirred on his shelf and flew to Skylar's shoulder.

Teir opened the door and walked in. He looked better than he had when Skylar and Gal had found him, but he still appeared a lot older than he should. His face wasn't as drawn and wrinkled, but there were still premature lines there. His hair was always going to be white, unless he colored it. Ms. Comely, the nurse for the students on Aduncus Island, said he would be fit in a few months. It was going to take a while for the side effects of his changes to not show on him so much.

"Del wanted me to come tell you we should be ready to fly in about half an hour. If you want some breakfast, you've got time to get it." Teir stared up at Skylar who was still sitting on the edge of his bunk.

His face was so changed, Skylar was still learning to read it, and he was trying his best to not read much of his friends' emotions and thoughts since they broke the gestalt on the island. He wanted more time to his own thoughts, and didn't want to burden them with the morass of dark depression he was struggling not to fall into. All the parties weren't helping. He was amazed by how easy the Tursiops found excuses for celebration.

"Thanks." Skylar slid off his bunk. He didn't feel like eating. Since they had gotten back, he'd managed to eat enough to keep going, but couldn't bring himself to enjoy it. "Are you getting settled in?"

Teir nodded. "Yeah. I'm glad Mom's letting me stay. I just don't think I belong on Hummassa anymore. I'm too different from everyone there."

"It takes some getting used to, but you'll find your stride." Skylar walked over to his mirror and ran a brush through his bed-mussed brown hair. He tried getting away with not bothering about that the first day back and Solaria had told him he looked like something the cat dragged in and promptly smoothed his hair down before ordering him back to his room to take a shower and come back looking decent.

"It might be easier without Mom here," Teir said. "I just hope she gets back on her feet helping with the rebuilding on Hummassa."

Skylar turned from the mirror and nodded. "Your mom's strong. She'll bounce back, and if she needs us, all she has to do is let us know and we'll be on the way." He managed a weak grin. "There are advantages to having our own starship."

"There are," Teir agreed. "How are you doing today?"

"Not looking forward to doing this," Skylar said.

"I hear you, but we'll all be with you." Teir patted his shoulder. "I don't know if I've said it yet, but your friends here are awesome. Sure, Solaria can be a bit scary, but she's loyal and fun. Del's great. I could've slept in the students' barracks, but he insisted I stay on Astara with you guys."

Skylar nodded and smoothed his shirt. He picked something nice for the day, a sleek blue shirt with the Stars' End logo on it. He always liked the fading star that made up the school's emblem. To him it represented the distance that needed to be traveled to get to knowledge.

Teir also wore a Stars' End shirt, although Skylar wondered if something other than blue would've gone better with his deep red skin.

"We're all hoping that being close with us will help you settle into your new life more easily. Being a psychic is a lot different from how we were brought up." Skylar walked to the door. Filzbalm left his shoulder and flew down the hall.

"I know, and your friends are helping me see that even after everything the raiders put me through, there are still good things about being a psychic." Teir trailed Skylar slightly as they headed toward the main flight deck.

"A lot of good things," Skylar said, his mood lightening for the first time in days, even if they did have a grim task ahead of them. "Maybe one of these days we'll be able to show you more of them."

"More of what?" Solaria asked as she came up the ramp into the ship, Leonada, Click and Yul with her.

"Good things about being a psychic." Skylar stopped and stared at them. "You don't all have to be here for this."

Solaria walked up and hugged him. She'd been overly supportive, but not majorly pushy about it since they returned from the Boarisk island. "We don't, but we are. You don't have to do this with just the five of you, although I doubt Astara will be leaving the ship when you get there."

"You are correct, Solaria," Astara said from the short hall that led to the flight deck. "I shall remain with the ship to make sure everything is ready for your departure."

Skylar let go of Solaria and stepped back. He glanced at the others who'd come on board with her. "I really do appreciate all of you coming."

"We were all there," Click said. "Not to mention he was our friend too."

"I wish I had come back and been of help," Yul said, looking sadder than the others. "But they needed someone to move the crate once we got it to the island. It hurts losing friends."

With that simple word, Skylar realized what had been at the heart of his despair over losing Gal. Although he'd only known the man for a few hours, he'd already become more of a friend than just an extra mover Click had found to help with the mission. Skylar didn't like saying goodbye to friends.

"I'm ready for takeoff," Astara said. "If everyone will find seats in the galley. Skylar, Del's waiting for you."

"Okay." He turned and started to walk away, then stopped. "Teir, Solaria, you two want to join us on the flight deck?"

Solaria glanced at Teir and nodded. "Sure."

As they walked toward the front of the ship, Skylar realized Solaria and Leonada had also worn their Stars' End finest. They all looked like they were representing the school, or like they were all part of the same ship's crew, which they were. He wondered if maybe they should think about designing something for Astara's crew. They wouldn't be students forever, but he felt they were all going to be part of the crew for years. He just hoped he wasn't going to be saying goodbye to any more of them any time soon.

Melody stood next to Del's chair, or rather her hologram did. She was still at her other school, the one her parents felt was more appropriate than the scattered remnants of Stars' End.

Filzbalm was already on the back of Skylar's customary seat.

"Don't you all look spiffy?" Melody asked.

"We should make a good impression, I think," Skylar said, taking the copilot's chair.

Del was also in Stars' End blue. "And we will. You know we really don't have to do this. They've already been told."

Skylar nodded. "I know. But this is going to make me feel better. I really appreciate everyone going with me…us."

Astara walked over and stood between Del and Skylar. There was a soft click as her avatar's body locked into place on ther deck plates. "Ramp is up and we're ready to fly."

"Follow the course we laid in earlier," Del said.

The ship barely shook as it rose from the hangar and maneuvered into the sky.

They weren't going into space, and flying over the oceans wasn't exactly what Skylar was in the mood for, but he did his best to enjoy the short flight that was over within minutes.

Astara came in low alongside Peni Island. There were several low houses near the shore, and a couple of ships were parked outside the hangar. Skylar recognized *The Deep Diver*, the Aduncus family ship. Astara eased her way over next to it, then set down in a puff of sand.

Skylar wished the trip had been longer. He unbuckled his seatbelt, stood and squared his shoulders. "Let's do this."

The others stood.

"We're right behind you." Del said.

Filzbalm settled into a comfortable position on Skylar's shoulder. *"We'll always be with you."*

Skylar scratched Filzbalm's head as they walked toward the ramp. "Thanks."

As they passed through the galley, the others rose and fell into line behind them. The air as they walked down the ramp and onto the beach was decidedly grim.

The inside of the main Peni house was fairly simple, like most of the Tursiops dwellings on Aduncus Island. The furniture was simple plascrete creations that didn't show much signs of wear. The floor was sand, letting the house flow easily from the beach. Most of the massive windows were open, allowing a steady breeze to blow in from the ocean, just a few feet away.

At the far end of the room stood an unmoving hologram of Gal. He looked young, happy and very much alive. A knot tightened in Skylar's chest. He hadn't been expecting that. Gal's body had never been recovered after the battle.

The room was full of people, mostly standing in small groups talking quietly. As Skylar and crew walked in, several of the closer groups stopped talking and stared at them. That was when Skylar realized there weren't many non-Tursiops there. Standing out like that didn't make him feel any better about the situation.

A Tursiops woman with the long elegant dress of a matron who Skylar had never met came over. "You must be Skylar and the crew of Astara. Welcome."

Del stepped to Skylar's side. "Gelendara, we are deeply saddened by this loss."

She nodded slowly. "We all are, Del. We all are." It was clear the woman was Gal's mother.

"Allow me to introduce those you might not know." Del quickly made introductions.

Nearby, someone beat a drum, and the Tursiops milling around the room instantly became silent. As soon as everyone took their seats, Gal's final services began.

Skylar sat there quietly with his friends around him as Gal's friends and family said kind, gentle and glowing things about him. Every word tightened his stomach. Then it was his turn to get up and speak.

It was all he could do to rise and walk up to the front of the room. Standing there with Gal's hologram looking over his shoulder made Skylar wonder if the projection was supposed to be larger than Gal had been in real life. Then he remembered how large he'd thought Gal to be when they first met.

With everyone in the room staring at him, Skylar forced himself to begin the tale of Gal's final adventure. He did his best to keep it direct, but he still ended up being the one who talked the longest.

THE SUN was setting, spreading flames across the water, by the time the service finally ended and Skylar and his friends were able to leave. It had been one of the hardest things he'd ever done, and something he didn't want to do again.

Solaria and Leonada walked on either side of him and he felt like they were herding him into a trap, or something.

"You did a very good job back there," Solaria said. "You made sure that none of them ever view Gal as anything but the hero he was."

"Thanks," Skylar mumbled.

Del touched Skylar's shoulder. "We were talking amongst ourselves. Click and Yul think Gal would like a bonfire. Do you want to do that here, or back at home?"

Nearby a ship lifted off, scattering sand around them as more of the service guests headed back to their own islands.

"He spent more time here than on Aduncus Island, didn't he?" Skylar really just wished they could go home and everyone would leave him alone for a while, but he wasn't going to leave until the very end. He was going stay there for Gal.

"Yeah," Click said from somewhere behind Skylar. "I mean he came over for parties and such, but not as much just to hang out."

"Where would we get the wood?" Skylar asked, still not feeling like it, but knowing it might help Click and Yul deal with the loss.

"I know where the family stashes drift wood," Yul said before dashing off.

"Okay," Skylar said. "Where do we need to go."

"Just head down the beach," Click said. "We'll get the wood and join you. Stop wherever feels right."

"Come on." Solaria took Skylar's arm and steered him away from Astara as Click and Yul dashed away.

Skylar sighed. "Why are people asking my opinion on this first?"

"You're our leader," Solaria said. "We didn't really talk about it, but you're the take-charge kinda guy."

Unsure what to say, Skylar kept walking. He hadn't set out to become their leader, but was sliding into the position fairly easily. He didn't mind, as long as he didn't send more of his friends to their deaths.

He wasn't sure what or when their next adventure would be, but the galaxy was changing around them. He wanted to be ready for whatever life threw at them, and if things were quiet until they graduated from Stars' End, that would suit him just fine. During that time, they'd decide what they wanted to do. He was still leaning toward finding a place in Intergal Rescue and working like Solaria's Uncle Phil did, traveling around saving people. But he also wanted to explore the galaxy and beyond. There were so many choices, but with his friends at his side, he was going to make the right ones and do his best to ensure they all had long, happy lives.

Skylar's adventures continue in,
"Skylar Mars and the Big Game".

If you'd like to stay on top of new releases and upcoming work by Drew Seren, please join our mailing list at www.drewseren.com.
And if you enjoyed Skylar's adventure, please leave a review. It's easy and won't take you very long.